CW00705790

'I won't *intrude* on your spare time any longer, Penny.'

James sat behind the wheel, staring impassively ahead. Penny, her words flung back at her so cruelly, struggled with a conflict of emotions.

'James——' What was there to say? Her pride hadn't completely deserted her—she wasn't going to plead with him to think well of her. The only thing to do was to get out of the car and walk away. She didn't look back—if she had she might have seen James slam his fists against the steering-wheel in despair.

70p

Dear Reader

RAW DEAL is second in Caroline Anderson's trilogy, in which Maggie is manipulated by her grandmother into discovering appearances can deceive. We go to Australia for Lilian Darcy's A PRIVATE ARRANGEMENT, where Belinda Jones cares for a pregnant diabetic—problems! Clare Mackay unfolds SISTER PENNY'S SECRET, in her second novel, and Elizabeth Petty returns with THE SURGEON FROM FRANCE, where a delightful old patient plays matchmaker. Have fun!

The Editor

Clare Mackay trained as an SRN in London before taking a break from nursing to raise a family. Having written stories as a hobby for many years, she decided to combine her interests and began writing Medical Romances. With her children now growing up, Clare has returned to nursing and uses her own experience in a busy general hospital, together with information gleaned from relatives in the medical profession, as background for her writing. She lives in Wiltshire.

Recent titles by the same author:

LEARNING TO CARE

SISTER PENNY'S SECRET

BY

CLARE MACKAY

MILLS & BOON LIMITED
ETON HOUSE   18–24 PARADISE ROAD
RICHMOND   SURREY   TW9 1SR

All the characters in this book have no existence outside the imagination of the Author, and have no relation whatsoever to anyone bearing the same name or names. They are not even distantly inspired by any individual known or unknown to the Author, and all the incidents are pure invention.

All Rights Reserved. The text of this publication or any part thereof may not be reproduced or transmitted in any form or by any means, electronic or mechanical, including photocopying, recording, storage in an information retrieval system, or otherwise, without the written permission of the publisher.

This book is sold subject to the condition that it shall not, by way of trade or otherwise, be lent, resold, hired out or otherwise circulated without the prior consent of the publisher in any form of binding or cover other than that in which it is published and without a similar condition including this condition being imposed on the subsequent purchaser.

First published in Great Britain 1992 by Mills & Boon Limited

© Clare Mackay 1992

Australian copyright 1992 Philippine copyright 1993 This edition 1993

ISBN 0 263 77982 3

Set in 10 on 11½ pt Linotron Plantin 03-9301-55913

Typeset in Great Britain by Centracet, Cambridge Made and printed in Great Britain

CHAPTER ONE

'I'M SO glad you're here, Penny. I don't know what I would have done without you.' Margaret Lambert settled more snugly into the pile of pillows on the sofa, and smiled up at her granddaughter.

Penny laughed. 'What an old fraud you are, Gran! You don't really need me to nurse you. You just wanted to wangle your way out of hospital early!' She grinned at her grandmother, who nodded in agreement.

'I hate those places. If I'd been in there any longer they'd have been carrying me out in a box!'

'Gran!' Penny shook her head in resignation. 'What have you got against hospitals? You seemed so pleased when I decided to become a nurse——'

'Well, it's a good career, if you like that sort of thing. I can't deny that we *need* hospitals, but that doesn't make me like being *in* them!'

'They saved your life—you know that, don't you?'

'Yes, I suppose so. The staff were all very good to me—but you can't beat being in your own home!'

'You'd better get some rest now—I don't think you slept much last night, did you?' Penny pulled the blanket a little higher over Margaret's bony shoulders.

'No, you're right. I feel quite tired now. . .'

Leaving her to doze by the fire, Penny went into the kitchen and began to prepare soup for their supper that evening. Her grandmother was still rather frail after her bad bout of pneumonia, and Penny tried hard to tempt her appetite with light and attractive meals. While she chopped vegetables she listened to a play on the radio, and was so deeply absorbed that the firm double rap on the front door was an unwelcome intrusion.

A succession of neighbours had called during the two days that Penny had been staying at Marsh Farm Cottage, and she flung open the door expecting to see another stalwart of Fernhill village clutching a spray of flowers or a jar of home-made preserves. Instead she was confronted by a tall, athletic figure, clad in a well-cut tweed jacket and dark grey trousers, and holding an unmistakable black case.

'I'm Dr Yorke—I've come to see how Mrs Lambert is getting on. . .

Penny stood almost transfixed in the doorway, gazing up at the doctor, who towered over her petite figure. He had the most remarkable voice, deep and smooth— *seductive* was the word that popped into Penny's head. The stern set of his strong jaw was offset by the amusement in his blue eyes as he waited to be admitted to the house.

'Do you think I could come in?' he asked after a couple of moments.

Penny blushed, suddenly aware that she had been staring. 'Of—of course,' she stammered, wiping her still damp hands on the back of her jogging trousers and standing back to admit the doctor to the little hallway. 'But I'm afraid,' she added, coming to her senses at last, 'my grandmother is asleep at the moment. I don't think she should be disturbed. . .

A flicker of irritation passed over Dr Yorke's face. 'I ought to see her, Miss—er. . .?'

'Penny Lambert. I'm staying with Gran for a week or so.'

'Well, as I was saying, Miss Lambert,' continued the doctor, 'I ought to see my patient this afternoon. This is my first visit since she was discharged from hospital.'

'I'm sorry, Doctor, but I think it's more important that she gets her rest. She doesn't sleep well at night, and she won't take any sleeping pills, so if she can get some rest during the day I consider it essential to let her do so. . .'

Penny drew herself up to her full height, which, being only an inch or two over five foot, did not seem very impressive beside this powerful man. But she was determined to stand her ground, so she looked the doctor squarely in the eye. For a moment they stood facing one another, Penny's warm hazel eyes holding an unspoken challenge.

Dr Yorke cocked an eyebrow slightly, and his mouth took on a rigid, angry line. 'I hope you realise, Miss Lambert, that you're not only wasting my time, but also risking your grandmother's health by your stubborn attitude. I'll call again this evening—and I expect to be able to see my patient!'

'I'm sure this evening will be more convenient, Doctor.' Penny's voice was carefully controlled to avoid any hint of amusement which, she knew, would only serve to enrage the doctor even more. She had no wish to cause ill feeling, but she couldn't understand why the common sense of her decision did not seem obvious to Dr Yorke.

'Oh,' she added, as she saw him out of the front door, 'I nearly forgot—the antibiotics are causing a rash— that's one of the reasons Gran doesn't sleep well at the moment. Perhaps she could have an antihistamine——'

The doctor's face clouded ominously. 'I'd be grateful if you'd leave the diagnostics and prescribing to me, young lady—that is, when I can actually get to see my patient! I'll be here at seven. Just make sure Mrs Lambert is awake this time. . .!'

Penny watched the man depart down the path, his

back rigid with fury. What an arrogant, self-opinionated. . . She shook her head in exasperation. Doctors!
She had had her fill of them—it would suit her fine if
she never met another doctor for the rest of her life!

Sure enough, at seven sharp the rap at the door
announced Dr Yorke's return. Margaret Lambert had
been amused to hear of Penny's run-in with 'young Dr
James', as she called him, but had issued a word or two
of warning about antagonising people in so small a
village.

'Does he live in Fernhill, then?' Penny had asked.

'No—but word gets around in a place like this, and
everyone's very fond of young Dr James.' Penny's
grandmother flashed her a knowing look. 'One or two
are more than just fond! He's not married—and he'll be
quite a catch for someone one of these days!'

'Well, whoever lands that particular cold fish has my
sympathy,' Penny had retorted.

Now, as she opened the front door once again to the
man in question, she experienced the same little ripple
of surprise which had caught her off guard before. Was
it something to do with the way his hair, so dark it was
almost black, curled a little at the back of his neck? Or
was it the open, enquiring look in his eyes as he turned
on the front step to face her?

Getting a grip on herself, she ushered him through the
door immediately, and without any further delay sent
him through to see his patient. She left them alone,
knowing that if there was anything important to report
about her grandmother's condition the doctor would
speak to her before he left.

She made coffee while she waited, watching the dark,
rich liquid dripping through the filter into the glass jug
below.

The latch lifted on the sitting-room door and Penny looked up, just in time to see Dr Yorke emerge from the room and glance around the hallway, obviously looking for her.

He spotted her through the open kitchen door and in two long strides was in the room, sniffing appreciatively. 'What a marvellous smell!'

'Yes, isn't it!' agreed Penny. 'I brought this Italian coffee down with me from London.'

'Good idea! I don't suppose the village shop has quite reached such levels of sophistication yet!' The doctor smiled again, and Penny busied herself with the coffee, not sure whether he was taking a dig at her or not.

'Have you time to have a cup?' she asked, hesitating with the jug in her hand. She half hoped he would refuse.

There was a moment's pause before the doctor nodded. 'I'd love some coffee. Your grandmother was my last call this evening—unless I'm paged by my answering service, of course.'

'So how do you think Gran's getting on, Dr Yorke?' asked Penny.

'She's doing very well. And please, call me James,' he smiled, taking the steaming cup from her hand and sitting down at the kitchen table. He leaned back in the chair and stretched his long legs under the table. Penny took a surreptitious look at him—he appeared somehow constrained in his conservative clothes. Despite the excellent quality and fit, the casual jacket and tie looked as if they belonged to someone else. Penny could imagine James Yorke looking far more at home in sports gear— his skin had a healthy colour which hinted at an easy summer tan. He should be striding along a wide, sandy beach with a surfboard under his arm. . . Suddenly she was reminded of another man on another beach, and she shut the image from her mind. With a huge effort she dragged herself back to the present to listen to what James was saying. . .

'You were right about the antibiotics—your grandmother isn't tolerating them well. But all the latest test results are negative, so I've stopped all her medication. What she needs now is good food, rest, gentle exercise, and she'll be fine!'

'That's wonderful,' smiled Penny. 'Well, I'll be here for as long as she needs me, so I'll be able to stop her doing too much too soon.'

'Yes. . .' James cleared his throat and looked a little awkward. 'I—er—Mrs Lambert told me you're a staff nurse. I wish you'd mentioned it this afternoon. I think I owe you an apology.'

'Apology accepted, but I can't see why it should make any difference. I think my opinion should have counted with or without a nursing qualification.'

'You're right. I'm afraid you just caught me at a bad moment. I came here this afternoon straight from a call where someone had followed the advice of an ignorant friend instead of the doctor, with serious consequences for the patient!'

'That sounds awful,' Penny agreed. 'But should you let a frustrating case like that cloud your judgement of other relatives and carers?'

'No. You're absolutely right, Miss Lambert. I consider myself reprimanded!' He gave her a teasing smile, and drained the last of his coffee.

Penny stood up to refill his cup, but was interrupted by a loud repetitive bleeping noise.

'Damn!' James frowned and reached into his pocket to switch off the bleep. 'I'm being paged—there must be an emergency. May I use your phone?'

'Of course—it's in the hall.'

She watched him stride towards the telephone, and heard his voice, low and decisive, as he spoke to his answering service.

Putting down the receiver, he turned to her with a resigned shrug. 'Thanks for the coffee, Penny. I'll have to go and see this patient. I'll call on your grandmother again next week—if there are any problems in the meantime, you can ring me.' His tone was brisk and businesslike, and Penny suddenly felt a tiny prick of disappointment that he was having to leave so abruptly.

'I suppose you'll be going back to London as soon as Mrs Lambert is back on her feet?' James asked, stooping to pick up his bag.

'Yes, I suppose I will.' Penny had no intention of telling this man that she had nothing to go back to—no job, no flat, no. . .lover. She didn't even like admitting to herself that she had no idea of what to do when she left the cosy, undemanding surroundings of the cottage and the village. There was nothing to return to— whatever she did next would be a fresh start, but as yet she didn't feel ready to make any decisions as to when or where this fresh start should take place.

James was by the door now, and Penny kept her thoughts to herself, merely returning his brief 'good-night' before closing the door behind him.

She looked in on her grandmother. It was time she went up to bed and tried to get a decent night's sleep.

Margaret was half dozing by the log fire. 'Oh, Penny——' She awoke with a start. 'Has young James gone?'

'Yes—he was called out to another patient.' Penny kept her voice deliberately neutral, knowing of old her grandmother's passion for matchmaking. A handsome, single GP, an unmarried granddaughter—how could she resist?

She was right—there was a twinkle in Margaret Lambert's faded blue eyes as she gathered up her magazines and knitting and prepared to go upstairs. 'What do you think of James?' she asked. 'Did you talk to him?'

'Yes, I talked to him—a little. We—we had a cup of coffee before he was called away.'

'And. . .?' prompted her grandmother.

'And nothing. If you really want to know, I think he has far too high an opinion of himself. He seems to think that being a doctor gives him some godlike quality which reduces everyone else to being incapable of having an intelligent thought.'

Margaret was not put off. 'But he's such a good-looking boy, don't you think?'

'Not particularly,' lied Penny. 'And he's hardly a boy, Gran!'

'He's thirty-four.'

'How do you know?'

'I asked.' Margaret chuckled, and Penny couldn't hide a grin. That was so typical of the old lady—if she wanted to know something, she would just come right out and ask.

'I wouldn't be too quick to dismiss him, Penny,' said her grandmother, as if Penny was considering the doctor for some sort of employment. 'He might seem a bit brash at first, but he's earned the respect of most of the people round here, and they're not renowned for their acceptance of newcomers. Old Dr Westlake was here for donkey's years, and when he died last year he left a gap which I thought would be very hard to fill. James Yorke had a tough job on his hands to win the approval of a community like this. I admire him—he's got all those old girls down at the Women's Institute eating out of his hand.'

'Gran!' admonished Penny. 'Those "old girls" are the same age as you——'

'Younger, most of them. . .' interrupted her grandmother.

'—and,' continued Penny, 'you know you love the WI meetings.'

'True. Now, help me up those stairs, and then I'll be all right. . .'

Later, tucked in bed with an electric blanket keeping her warm, Mrs Lambert looked fondly at her granddaughter.

'You know, you don't have to hang around here, Penny. I'm so much better—you ought to be out getting yourself another job. I worry about you.'

Penny perched on the edge of the bed and took the old lady's hand in her own. 'I love being here, Gran. I'm in no hurry to get a job—I've got a bit of money saved. I'd like to stay on for a couple of weeks.'

'Of course. Stay as long as you like.' Mrs Lambert squeezed Penny's hand and settled more comfortably into the bed.

Penny went to her own room and pottered about for a while before she too went to bed. Lying in the quiet darkness, staring up at the ceiling with its undulating surface sliced in half by a heavy beam of ancient blackened oak, she found herself thinking once more about the tall, self-assured man who had twice whisked in and out of the cottage in the space of one day. She couldn't deny that he had made an impression on her—but not the same impression he seemed to make on his adoring patients!

Penny was out the next time James called. She returned from a shopping trip to find her grandmother washing up two coffee mugs.

'You've just missed young Dr James,' she announced as soon as Penny came through the door.

'Oh?' Penny's first thought was that he might have been annoyed to find her grandmother alone.

'You'll be pleased to hear that he's pronounced me quite clear of the pneumonia. As long as I'm sensible, there's no need for me to be treated like an invalid any more.'

'Which means. . .?' Penny frowned slightly.

'That you mustn't feel you have to stay and look after me. You can go and look for a job, Penny.'

Penny thought for a moment. 'Yes,' she said at last, 'I suppose I'd better find something soon. My money won't last forever. But, Gran——'

'What is it, dear?'

'Do you think—would it be all right if I stayed here while I apply for jobs? I haven't really got anywhere else to go at the moment.'

'What happened to your flat?' asked Margaret.

'I gave up the flat when I handed in my notice.'

'But you never told me. . . I don't know what happened in London, Penny, and I'm not going to pry into your business, but you know you can always talk to me if you want to, don't you?' The old lady looked concerned.

Penny put a reassuring arm around her and gave her grandmother a hug. 'I know, Gran. There's nothing much to tell. It was—a romance that turned sour. I was so fed up that I wanted to get away completely, so I gave up the flat. Perhaps it was a bit rash, because it means I've dumped myself on you. . .'

'Darling, don't worry. This is your home for as long as you want. By the way. . .' Margaret's voice became over-casual '. . .James was asking about you. He wanted to know if you'd gone back to London—he seemed to be under the impression that you were still working there.'

'Oh?' Penny didn't sound very interested.

'I told him you'd be around for a few days yet. If he wanted to see you. . .'

Penny glared at her grandmother, before breaking into helpless laughter. 'You're incorrigible, Gran!' she gasped at last.

The following day, Friday, was market day in Ellminster. Penny drove the three miles from Marsh Farm Cottage to the town in her red Mini, enjoying the weak spring sunshine. It was still rather chilly, but already there were daffodils in the gardens she passed, and that feeling of optimism in the air which only spring could create—a promise of good things to come.

She parked carefully in a huge car park behind the new shopping precinct, and briskly walked through a maze of side streets to the old market place. This town held special memories for her, of childhood holidays spent with her grandparents. In those days, when her grandfather had been alive, he and Gran had run Marsh Farm together, and for a treat she would be allowed to come to Ellminster with Grandpa when he was buying or selling sheep at market. Now all that was left of Marsh Farm was her grandmother's cottage—the rest had been sold off—and the open-air livestock markets in Ellminster had long since gone. Little remained unchanged except these colourful stalls every Friday, selling everything imaginable from vegetables to compact discs. Today Penny started with her usual stroll around, taking in the sounds and smells, before she filled her shopping basket with the fruit and vegetables she needed for the weekend's meals.

'Hello again!' A voice behind her made her jump, and she wheeled round to find James Yorke smiling at her as if they were old friends. His confident approach irritated her quite unreasonably, and she found herself snapping at him. 'Do you have to creep up on people like that? You almost made me drop all my shopping!'

His smile faded, and his tone became a little sarcastic. 'Oh, I'm sorry—I didn't know you were of such a nervous disposition. Here, let me help. . .'

He tried to hold open her basket while she jammed in her paper bags bulging with apples and oranges, but somehow between them all they managed to do was tip half the fruit on to the pavement, where it rolled away under the market stall.

'Now look! It's ruined!' wailed Penny, feeling foolish and wishing she had never set eyes on 'young Dr James'.

'My fault entirely. I'll get you some more.' James's voice was clipped, and he stepped forward to the stall-holder and ordered more fruit.

'No, James, I can't let you buy that for me—it wasn't your fault. . .'

'Yes, it was. Put this in your basket, and don't say another word!' He sounded angry, and almost forced the paper bag into Penny's hands before striding away across the market place. She stood for a moment, watching his straight back as he walked away from her. She could tell that he was annoyed, and she wavered between resentment at his attitude and guilt that her less than welcoming greeting had led to this trouble.

Suddenly she made a snap decision and started after him, almost running to catch up with the man whose long stride was carrying him further and further away. At the other side of the square he had to pause for a car to pull out, giving Penny a chance to make up the distance between them.

'James——'

At the sound of her breathless voice James turned his

head and looked down at her, his face expressionless, guarded.

'James, it's my turn to apologise. Thank you for buying the fruit. . .'

He inclined his head in acknowledgement, but didn't speak. Penny, lost for words, licked her lips and ran a hand nervously through her cropped fair hair.

James gazed at her silently, as she stood on the edge of the pavement, the awkwardness of the situation bringing a slight blush to her pale cheeks. Her tiny figure looked fragile, and he fought hard against an urge to sweep her up in his arms. There was something in her eyes—a deep, hidden pain which he wanted to ease away.

'Well, I'll just—um——' Penny started to back away, feeling foolish. It had been a mistake to run after him like this—the contemptuous silence made it plain that James Yorke had no more time for her. 'Goodbye, James.' She turned on her heel.

'Will you have dinner with me this evening—that is, if you're free?'

Penny couldn't believe her ears. She wheeled round to face the doctor again, a sharp retort on her lips, but she was unprepared for the warm, open smile which confronted her.

'Please don't refuse—this is the first night off I've had all week. If you don't come I shall have to spend the evening totally alone in my empty house. . .'

His voice was teasing and persuasive. Penny frowned. 'Oh, James, I don't think. . .'

'Actually, there's something I particularly want to talk to you about. Come on, Penny—your grandmother will be fine without you for one evening!'

She took a deep breath. 'Yes, all right, I'll have dinner with you.'

'Good. I'll collect you at seven-thirty.'

Once again Penny experienced a strange excitement in the pit of her stomach as she watched James stride across the road to his car, but as soon as he had driven off she began to regret her impulsive decision. She hardly knew James Yorke, and they hadn't exactly hit it off on the brief occasions they had met. Why on earth was she going to spend the evening with the man—and what could he possibly want to discuss with her?

CHAPTER TWO

JAMES sat back in his chair and sighed contentedly. 'I'd almost forgotten what it was like to have time off! I'm glad you allowed yourself to be talked into coming this evening, Penny!'

Across the restaurant table his eyes held hers for a moment in a disturbingly intimate look. Penny hoped that in the dim light of the bistro her blush would not be noticeable.

James appeared far more comfortable this evening in casual cotton trousers and a crisp striped shirt, the collar unbuttoned to reveal a strong, muscular neck. His skin looked as if it would be smooth and cool to touch, and Penny, realising where her thoughts were leading her, almost blushed again.

After her initial misgivings about spending the evening with James, she had welcomed the opportunity to abandon her customary jeans and sweatshirt, and had donned a short skirt and fitted, short-sleeved linen jacket. She had made up her face with care, and had been rewarded by the appreciative smile with which James had greeted her on his arrival at Marsh Farm Cottage.

He watched her now as she sipped her wine. Her tiny figure looked slighter than ever in the tailored outfit, and with her short hair falling in a tousled fringe across her forehead, she made him think of a little sprite. Somehow, magically, she had entered his life—the problem was, how to keep her there?

'Tell me about yourself,' he said casually. 'Where did you train—in London?'

'Yes—at the Royal Western. That's where I've been staffing too.'

James raised his eyebrows and laughed. 'What a coincidence—that's where I did my medical training! So did my brother, Kit—he's still working there!'

'Really? Goodness!' Penny grinned. 'So you must know Sister Montgomery—I've been working on her ward. . .'

'Monty?' James rolled his eyes and roared with laughter. 'The woman terrified the life out of us new housemen! Mind you, she taught me more about diabetes than I had managed to pick up in medical school. I owe a lot to dear old Monty. She was the one who fired my interest in the condition—now I'm trying to build up a proper service for our diabetic patients in the practice.'

Penny sat forward. 'That sounds interesting. What proportion of your patients are diabetic?'

She listened, absorbed, while James explained his plan to offer more GP-based help to the patients with long-term medical problems.

'That brings me on to the reason I said I wanted to speak to you this evening,' he said at last. 'I've heard you're looking for a job.'

The blunt statement took her by surprise. 'What— who told you that?' she spluttered.

He looked slightly sheepish. 'Well, your grandmother mentioned——'

'Gran!' She shook her head in exasperation before looking sharply at James, who was watching her with more than a hint of amusement. 'I still don't see what my employment situation has to do with you. . .'

'I'm offering you a job—albeit a temporary one.'

'What kind of job?'

'Jan O'Connell, our practice nurse, is off sick, and likely to be for some time. She's pregnant, and having a few problems, so I think it will be at least two months before she's back—if at all. Would you be interested in filling in for her, even for just a few weeks, while you're looking around for something permanent?'

Penny was taken aback by this sudden suggestion. 'But—but I don't know anything about general practice. I'm not experienced in community nursing. . .'

'We're a small practice—and there's always one of us on the premises to help you out,' James told her. 'The district nurses do all the home nursing—you'd be running the treatment-room in the surgery, doing dressings, taking blood samples, health promotion—that sort of thing. We've been managing without a nurse at all for the last month, and things are getting pretty chaotic. It would really help if you could come in and take some of the work off our hands!'

'Oh, James, I don't know. . .' Penny sounded doubtful. The idea, now that it had been raised, certainly interested her. It would be a new area of nursing, and one which, with its health promotion side, had a certain appeal—but there was James. She thought about their first encounter, and the way the sparks had flown over her grandmother's treatment. She suspected that he wouldn't be at all easy to work with.

'I'm not pressing you for a decision this evening.' James could see the doubt in her eyes. 'Think about it over the weekend, and on Monday you could come down to the surgery, meet my partner, and have a look at the place. No obligation to take the job!'

She nodded slowly. 'OK—that sounds like the best idea. But I'm not promising anything. . .'

'No, of course not. But I'm relieved you haven't dismissed the idea out of hand. Now, if you don't want more coffee, shall we go?'

Penny was quiet in the car on the way home. James

was a careful driver, and she had noticed in the restaurant that he had drunk only mineral water after an initial small glass of white wine. Her own glass, however, had miraculously refilled itself more than once, and now she sat enveloped in a warm and comforting glow.

Outside Marsh Farm Cottage James stopped the car and silenced the engine. For a couple of minutes they both sat, taking in the absolute quiet of the night. At last Penny sighed, and shifted in her seat, knowing that she must leave the comfort of the car, and the unexpectedly pleasant company of James.

'Thank you for this evening, James. I really enjoyed myself. . .' She turned, one hand on the door handle, and looked at her host. Her heart lurched as she realised that James Yorke was watching her very closely, very seriously, with clear, undisguised desire in his eyes.

'So did I, Penny.' His voice was husky, and he leaned forward a little to cup her face in his hand. She seemed rooted to the spot, transfixed by surprise. She knew that if he tried to force himself on her, their potential working relationship would be ruined, and what she had been considering on the way home to be a very interesting, if temporary new job would be out of the question.

She needn't have worried. Whatever she had seen, or thought she had seen, in James's eyes was well under control. He leaned across, planted a brief, sweet kiss on her cheek, and released her, leaving her wondering if she had imagined the look which had brought such a tremble to her limbs.

Deftly he sprang from the car and came around to help her out of the passenger seat. Walking with her to the front door of the cottage, he plunged his hands in his pockets and hung back a little.

'So you'll come to the surgery on Monday and have a look round?'

'Yes, I'll be there. But I'm not——

'I know! You're not promising anything!' James laughed, holding up his hands in mock self-defence. 'What a cautious person you are, Penny!' Still chuckling, he sauntered back to his car.

Penny let herself into the quiet cottage, brooding over his words. She hadn't always been cautious, and look what trouble she had brought upon herself!

Neil Westlake was a quietly spoken man with a rather harassed air about him, and Penny took to him immediately. He had joined his father's practice as, he told her, 'something to do while I made up my mind about specialising', and had never returned to hospital medicine. Now his father was dead, and Neil was running the practice. A deep love of his work shone in his face while she spoke, and Penny found herself, rather unfairly perhaps, comparing his gentle manner with the prickly treatment she had received on her first meeting with James Yorke. If she were ill, she thought, she knew which of the two doctors she would choose to visit her.

James had been called out to an emergency a couple of minutes after her arrival, so Neil showed her around the practice, which was accommodated in a converted Georgian house near the market place in Ellminster. What had once been the two front rooms and a spacious hallway had now been opened out to become the waiting-room and reception desk. Behind the desk were shelves holding row upon row of patient files, which Angela, the receptionist, seemed to know her way around with uncanny accuracy.

'We've got a practice manager who comes in every afternoon to sort out the budgeting and bureaucracy,' explained Neil, leading Penny through to the treatment-room which would be her domain.

The room was small and chaotic. Seeing Penny's expression as she looked around at the mess, Neil pulled a rueful face. 'I expect James told you that we've been struggling on without a nurse! I'm afraid we've left it a bit untidy, but I think you'll find that basically it's quite well equipped. Things have been so hectic lately. . .'

'So I see. It's difficult to know where to start.'

'Does that mean you'll come in and help us?'

'Well—if you think I'll be of any use. . .'

'Wonderful! Can you start tomorrow, by any chance?'

Morning surgery was due to start in ten minutes, and already Penny could hear the hum of voices in the waiting area as she stood in the middle of the treatment-room and tried to decide what to do first. The door burst open and James appeared.

'You're here already—fantastic! I'll buzz you on the internal phone if I've got a patient for you—all right?'

Without waiting for a reply he shot through the door in the direction of his room. Penny was left wondering what on earth was going to be thrown at her during the course of the morning.

She started by donning the white coat Neil had found for her, and launched in on clearing the muddle. Neil had been right—the treatment-room had been well planned, with cupboard space for everything, and before long the scattered dressing packs, instruments and syringes had been sorted out and returned to their rightful places. Once the room was tidy she took time to look at some of the health promotion literature which seemed to be in plentiful supply. Dietary advice, anti-smoking leaflets, immunisation recommendations—there was a lot to take in. The walls were covered with health education posters, and height and weight charts displayed above a set of scales reminded Penny that

James had talked of weight reduction clinics which the practice nurse had started before she went off sick.

She was beginning to wonder whether she had jumped into this job without giving it enough consideration, when the telephone on the desk rang. For a moment she stared at it before forcing herself to pick up the receiver. 'Yes?' she said tentativley.

'Can you take a couple of blood samples for me?' James voice was brisk.

'Er—yes, of course,' said Penny, looking around to make sure she knew where the necessary equipment was kept.

'Good—full blood count and cholesterol, please. I'm sending Mr Gregory through.'

Penny took a deep breath. Well, she was here to work, and it was no good getting cold feet now! Quickly she gathered together the necessary needle and blood bottles, together with a swab and tourniquet. She had been taught how to take a blood sample at the Royal, but as a rule it was the phlebotomists' job to go round the hospital obtaining the samples, so she wasn't very practised in the technique.

Mr Gregory was a portly grey-haired man in his early sixties, with a florid complexion which suggested a lifetime spent out of doors. He sat down and immediately rolled up his sleeve, a veteran of years of blood tests.

'I've been a farm worker all my life,' he told Penny as she strapped the tourniquet around his upper arm to distend the vein. 'I'd be working still, but I 'ad to give it up a couple o' years back,' he continued in his Cotswold burr. 'This damned hypertension, that's been my trouble all this time. My blood-pressure's been bad for more'n twenty year. My old mother was the same. Now that young doctor wants me to change all my diet, cut out this 'n that, fat and what 'ave you—at my time o' life!'

While she listened, Penny deftly filled both bottles, and now she held a cotton wool swab over the puncture site. 'Could you please press firmly on that while I fill in the form?' She made sure Mr Gregory was pressing on the right spot before moving away to write his details on the bottles and the laboratory form.

'You the new sister, then?' he enquired, looking her up and down.

'I'm just filling in while Sister O'Connell is away,' she explained.

'Oh? Where do you usually work, then?' Mr Gregory was in no hurry to leave the surgery, it seemed.

'London,' Penny answered, almost without thinking.

'London, eh? You goin' back, then?'

'I'm not sure. Probably.'

'That's a shame. Perhaps you'll change your mind when you've been here for a bit. I can't understand anyone wanting to live in a city!' Mr Gregory was rolling down his sleeve and preparing to leave. Picking up his cap, he stood up and made for the door. 'Right you are, my dear. Many thanks. I 'ope you'll be staying with us a bit longer.'

'Goodbye, Mr Gregory.' Penny smiled as she showed him out into the corridor. To her surprise, there was another patient sitting outside her room. 'Are you waiting for me?' asked Penny.

The thin nervous-looking woman jumped up. 'Yes. Dr Yorke sent me down for a blood test.' She thrust her notes into Penny's hand and followed her into the treatment-room. Penny looked at James's entry on the card—another FBC.

Once again she prepared her equipment, and looked for a suitable vein from which to take the blood sample.

To her dismay, even with the tourniquet in place, Mrs Palmer's veins were hard to see. Oh, well, thought Penny, there's got to be a vein in there somewhere—here goes! Gently she pushed in the needle, slotted on the vacuum bottle, and waited a couple of seconds—but nothing happened. She withdrew the needle slightly—still nothing. It was clear that she had missed the vein. Mrs Palmer was looking anxious, and Penny decided against having a second, probably fruitless attempt.

'I'm having trouble finding a vein, Mrs Palmer,' she said honestly. 'I think I'll have to ask Dr Yorke to come and take the sample.' Feeling foolish, she picked up the receiver and pressed the extension button for James's surgery.

'Yes?' The voice was clipped.

'I'm sorry, Dr Yorke—could you take this blood test for me? I'm having trouble. . .'

'I'll come in a minute!' He rang off, and Penny suppressed a sigh. He had sounded very impatient. Presumably he was thinking that perhaps she was going to be more trouble than she was worth.

'He'll be here shortly, Mrs Palmer,' smiled Penny.

'That's all right, Sister. It's best to get someone who knows what they're doing, isn't it?'

Penny felt completely deflated. 'Well, yes. . .' she muttered, wondering if the put-down had been deliberate or just a tactless remark. 'Dr Yorke is very experienced——'

The door flew open and James strode in, grabbed the clean needle Penny was proffering, and without a moment's hesitation slipped it into an invisible vein and drew the sample.

Mrs Palmer looked triumphantly at Penny as James dashed back to his surgery.

'He's marvellous, isn't he?' she asked, and Penny

attempted to nod and smile in agreement, all the time wishing she had never let James Yorke talk her into doing this damned job!

She was clearing away and checking the details on the lab forms when the phone buzzed again. This time it was Neil's soft voice on the end of the line. 'Can you syringe ears, Penny?'

Penny thought back a couple of years to a stint spent in an ENT outpatients' clinic, and smiled to herself. 'It's one of my areas of expertise!' she joked.

'Fine! I'm sending Mr Tiley along.'

The morning passed quickly. After dealing with Mr Tiley's ears, Penny dressed a minor burn, removed stitches from a head wound, made two blood-pressure checks and gave a tetanus booster. At eleven-thirty the door opened and James appeared bearing two cups of coffee.

'Thought you might be in need of this!' he said, setting her mug down on the desk in front of her before perching on the edge to drink his own.

'How's it going so far?' he asked, regarding her with a serious expression.

Penny pulled a face. 'One moment I think I'm enjoying it, and the next I wonder what I'm doing here. Mrs Palmer's blood test——'

'Don't worry about it. Jan can hardly ever manage to get anything out of her—she's got tiny veins. You get used to knowing just where to position the needle even if you can't see a vein under the skin.'

'Well, thanks a lot! If Jan finds her difficult, why did you send her to me?' asked Penny indignantly. 'You know I'm not very experienced at taking bloods!'

'I thought it was worth a try.' James grinned at her. 'And for all I knew you might have managed it without any trouble. OK, I promise I'll keep the difficult ones to myself for the time being—but I'm sure in a week or two you won't need any help. Any other problems so far?'

She shook her head, and he stood up. 'I'd better start my calls. I'm back for afternoon surgery at four o'clock. I think you've got a few people booked in for jabs and dressings and things now, haven't you?' Penny looked at her list and nodded.

'I don't know what you want to do this afternoon——' said James thoughtfully. 'We normally have a well woman clinic, but with Jan away we cancelled it for this week. There won't be any more patients in until evening surgery.'

'Perhaps I could spend the afternoon finding my way around all this paperwork. . .' suggested Penny.

'Wonderful idea! I must go—see you later!'

Picking up his cup and a pile of notes, James disappeared from the treatment-room, leaving Penny musing over how unexpectedly things could turn out. A few days ago she had been wondering just what she was going to do and where she was going to go—and now here she was, experiencing a new side of nursing, and able, for the first time in weeks and weeks, to immerse herself in work without being constantly reminded of Chris Freeman.

When the last of the morning patients had gone, Penny was able to take herself off into the town and do a little shopping to take home that evening. She bought sandwiches for lunch and ate them sitting behind the reception desk with Angela, who was a mine of information about the various quirks of both doctors. 'Neil is just like his father—a real softie,' she said, starting to demolish an enormous cream éclair. 'It's James you've got to watch out for! He's a perfectionist—everything's got to be done by the book, and he doesn't mind telling you if he thinks you're not up to scratch.'

'Thanks for warning me—I'll have to be on my guard!' Penny watched Angela wipe a stray speck of cream from the corner of her mouth, and wondered how she managed to remain as skinny as a rail.

'Oh, and you'll find Friday is your busiest day,' added Angela. 'All your leg ulcer ladies like to come in for their dressings on Fridays so that they can come to market at the same time and save on the bus fare.'

Penny laughed. 'That makes sense!'

Joan, the practice manager, arrived at two o'clock, and the next couple of hours were spent going through the necessary details for Penny's contract, and all the paperwork with which she would have to become familiar while she was working at the practice.

'It looks as if I have to fill in three forms every time I give an injection!' she sighed.

Joan looked sympathetic. 'I'm afraid so, but you'll soon get to know what's what. It's not as daunting as you might think.'

All too soon four o'clock arrived and the waiting-room filled once again. This time there were a lot of children with harassed-looking mothers, and Penny was kept busy for the next hour looking at ears, and sore fingers, and assorted spots and rashes. Officially she was supposed to finish at five-thirty, but it was nearly six before the waiting space outside the treatment-room cleared, and she was able to tidy away all her equipment.

She was pulling on her jacket when the telephone buzzed. James's extension light was flashing. With a weary sigh she picked up the receiver. 'Yes?'

'You're still here, then! You'll have to claim overtime! Have you got a minute before you go?'

'Yes, I'll come through.' Stifling her annoyance,

Penny took off her jacket again and crossed the corridor towards James's room. Perhaps he needed a chaperone for a female patient. She really wanted to get home and start cooking—Gran didn't like to eat too late in the evening; it made it difficult for her to sleep.

To her surprise James was alone. He pulled a face. 'My last patient hasn't arrived. I'll hang around for a while and see if he turns up, then start my calls. How have you enjoyed your day?'

Penny paused for a moment or two to think before replying. 'I've enjoyed it very much on the whole. I think I've got a lot to learn, but it's very satisfying work. I just hope I don't make too many mistakes.'

James clung back his head and roared with laughter. 'Good grief, are you always so deadly serious about everything? You need to relax, unwind. . .and I've got just the thing! What are you doing tomorrow evening?'

'Tomorrow? I—er——'

'Nothing? Good. I had a call from Jan O'Connell this afternoon, and she's invited us round for a spot of supper tomorrow. I'll ring back and accept.'

Penny was completely taken aback by the assumption that she would want to spend the evening with James and his friends. 'No, James!' On a rising tide of anger she faced him, eyes glittering. 'I'm afraid I object to having my social life organised for me! You'll just have to tell Jan that it wasn't convenient!'

James looked crestfallen. 'She'll be very disappointed—she's really looking forward to meeting you. I think she wants to tell you all the dire things about working for Neil and me—well, me mostly. She's always had a soft spot for Neil. They've known each other for years.'

Penny waited, silently, her anger still simmering.

'I think you'll like her,' continued James. 'She'll be able to give you far more help with this job than I can.'

'Then perhaps I can arrange to meet her in working time. . .'

'Oh, come on, Penny! Even though the girl's sick, she's been generous enough to invite us round, so that she can welcome you to Ellminster. Couldn't you be gracious enough to spare a couple of hours?'

The dig hit home. Penny's indignation was overlaid by guilt. 'Well, for Jan's sake, I'll come. But please, James, in future, don't intrude on my spare time!'

He narrowed his eyes and glared at her, his lips compressed into a tight, hard line. 'Thank you for the warning, Penny, but I assure you it wasn't necessary. You've made it perfectly plain that spending tomorrow evening together will be a duty rather than a pleasure!'

His voice was so cold that she gave an involuntary shiver. At that moment, from outside the door came a cough, followed by a tentative knock.

'Ah! My patient—at last!' James stood up and crossed the room, pausing for a moment to tower over Penny. His height suddenly seemed intimidating.

Without another word, she left the room, collected her shopping and jacket, and headed for home.

The evening seemed to drag interminably. She answered her grandmother's questions about the job as cheerfully as she could, but inwardly her heart sank at the thought of working alongside James again tomorrow. As for spending the evening in his company—she pushed the thought from her mind. The whole thing would be a disaster, she was sure. Why had she been weak enough to succumb to his emotional blackmail?

As she lay in bed, sleepless, she tried to sort her jumbled thoughts into some kind of order. Why was James Yorke causing so much turmoil in her mind?

Carefully she dissected each encounter she had had with the doctor. At last she could come to only one conclusion—that despite the fact that he was overbearing and insensitive, she found him physically very attractive. Well, there it was. Now that she had acknowledged the fact, she could begin to deal with it. The very last thing she wanted at the moment was another relationship—if she had learned one thing through the whole sorry affair with Chris, it was that she was better off on her own!

'I can't tell you how much better I feel knowing that someone's holding the fort!' Jan smiled warmly at Penny, but the dark shadows beneath her eyes belied her words. She clearly wasn't feeling well at all.

'I hope you don't mind too much if I ring you up in a panic every now and then!' Penny pulled a face, then laughed. 'There's such a lot to learn—it's so different from hospital nursing!'

'Oh, feel free to ring—in fact I'd welcome the chance to feel involved!' smiled Jan. 'I miss work like mad. I think I might go crazy by the time this baby's born!'

'No, you won't, love—I'll keep you sane somehow!' Steven O'Connell had appeared from the kitchen in time to hear his wife's comment, and now he leaned over the back of the sofa and planted a tender kiss on the top of her head.

She reached up and took his hand, pressing it to her cheek and giving him a weary smile. 'I know you will. I'm just having a moan!' She shifted uncomfortably on the sofa. 'It's having to lie around like this all the time— I feel useless. I should be doing all sorts of things, but no one will let me.'

'She thinks I'm behaving like a gaoler,' explained Steven, 'keeping her locked up in her cell all day!

Explain to her, will you, James? Knock a bit of sense into the woman's head!'

James merely shrugged. 'She's heard it all from her own doctor. If she rests, she should be fine. I know it's hard, Jan. But you want this baby so much, you've got to give it the best chance. . .'

'Oh, I know. And to tell the truth, I don't feel much like running about anyway. I'm still getting such dreadful sickness. I never dreamed pregnancy could feel so bad—I imagined myself blooming and beautiful, like in magazines! Why don't they ever show pictures of women looking like something the cat's dragged in?'

'Poor old Jan!' James was perched on the arm of the sofa, and now he ruffled her hair affectionately. 'You've been very unlucky, but I bet you in a couple of months you'll bloom like mad!'

'Or be blooming mad. . .' muttered Jan, with the ghost of a smile.

'Supper's ready, folks,' announced Steven, bringing a delicious-looking quiche through from the kitchen and putting it down on the low table in front of the sofa, where it was joined by hot crusty rolls and salads. 'This is about the limit of my culinary prowess—I hope you don't mind eating it on your knees? That way Madam can recline in splendour. . .'

'OK, OK, don't rub it in!' grumbled Jan.

'Steven, this quiche is wonderful!' Penny cut the flan into slices and put a piece on a plate for Jan. 'Did you make it yourself?'

'Well, yes. . .' Steven sounded bashful, and Jan interrupted.

'What he won't tell you, Penny, is that he's actually a very good cook. Unlike poor James there, who can't even managed to make his own coffee. . .' She gave James a wicked look, and winked at Penny.

'Oh, dear,' drawled Penny, taking her cue, 'that's a shame! Who *does* make your coffee for you, James?' She looked seriously at the doctor, who was steadfastly refusing to rise to the bait.

'Well, that's the problem!' Jan was enjoying herself. 'Apparently no one at the practice can find it mentioned in their job description. . .'

'All right, all right!' James shook his head in mock self-pity. 'What have I done to deserve this?'

'You'll notice him, Penny, at about eleven o'clock, wandering around the surgery looking pathetic, hoping someone will take pity on him. Ignore him—I always do.'

They all laughed. Steven gave James a brotherly pat on the shoulder. 'The only thing worse than a nurse, James old boy——' he paused, waiting for James to join in '—is two nurses!'

Penny and Jan ignored the gibe, and chattered on. Penny had taken immediately to this warm-hearted girl, and felt sorry that she wasn't able to enjoy her pregnancy as she should. But it was obvious that not much could curb Jan's exuberant spirits.

'Tell me about your job in London,' she said now. 'I can't imagine why you'd want to give it up and come to a sleepy place like this!'

'Oh, it makes a welcome change, I can assure you.' Penny chose her words carefully. She had no intention of telling anyone here the real reason for giving up her job, or her relief at getting away from London with all its associated memories. 'I felt I was becoming stale— I'd trained and worked in the same hospital for five years, and I wanted a change of scene. It was pure chance that brought me down here to look after Gran. Had I not given up my job, I wouldn't have been free to come and stay with her. . .'

'And you wouldn't have been landed with standing in for me! Have you got definite plans—I mean, if I do what Steven wants me to do and give up the idea of coming back to work, do you think you'd be interested in taking the job on permanently?' asked Jan.

Penny felt James's eyes upon her as she searched around for a suitable answer. 'Oh, I—it's probably a bit early to say, Jan. And it would really be up to Neil and James—they may think I'm hopeless. Let's wait and see. As far as I'm concerned, it's still your job.'

It was still quite early when they took their leave. Jan seemed very tired, and Penny noticed that James looked concerned as he kissed Jan goodbye.

He was quiet as he drove Penny home.

'Is Jan going to be all right?' she asked at last.

'If she stays off her feet for the time being, she's got a good chance of keeping that baby. Steven was telling me that the latest scan was fine, so it's a question of being patient. Not easy for someone like Jan.'

'No—she's a lively person, isn't she?' Penny thought for a minute. 'I like them both very much,' she added.

'So the duty wasn't too arduous, then?' James's voice held a note of sarcasm.

'No.' Remembering yesterday's argument, Penny felt a pang of remorse. 'I enjoyed myself,' she admitted.

He pulled up outside the cottage. 'Good,' he said simply. 'Well, I won't *intrude* on your spare time any longer, Penny. Goodnight.'

He sat behind the wheel, staring impassively ahead. Penny, her words flung back at her so cruelly, struggled with a conflict of emotions. The pleasant mood of the evening had been shattered, and with it the fragile barrier she had begun building to shield herself from the physical presence of James Yorke.

'James——' What was there to say? Her pride hadn't

completely deserted her—she wasn't going to plead with him to think well of her.

The only thing to do was to get out of the car and walk away. She didn't look back—if she had she might have seen James slam his fists against the steering-wheel in despair.

CHAPTER THREE

WELL, thought Penny grimly as she let herself into the treatment-room the following morning, let's just hope it's a busy day. If I'm tied up with a patient, at least I can't have another argument with James Yorke!

Her wish was granted—a steady stream of patients arrived at her door, and by the time she had finished for the morning, James had already gone out on his rounds.

'Dr Yorke left a message,' said Angela, coming in with a piece of paper. 'He said if you haven't anyone booked in this afternoon, would you like to go on a couple of over-seventy-five visits with him?'

Penny's heart sank. '*Have* I got anyone booked?' Before Angela could shake her head she knew what the answer would be.

'Yes—OK, I'll go with him. It should be interesting!' In more ways than one, she added silently.

James had already explained that all patients over seventy-five years of age were to be offered a health check every year, either in the surgery or at home. Penny knew that James and Neil wanted her to take over some of this work, but first she needed to become familiar with the type of problems she might encounter.

'It's often a question of listening carefully,' explained James as they drove to the first call. 'Some patients will drop little hints which you need to pick up on. They might not want to come straight out and tell you that they're having trouble with their waterworks, or even that they can't afford to have the heating on enough. You need to be careful about the way you ask questions.

38

Encourage the patient to talk, rather than just answer yes or no.'

They had arrived outside a neat white bungalow, and now James was striding up the path towards the front door, leaving Penny to follow.

'This is our new practice nurse, Sister Lambert,' he said, as they were ushered into the spotless little house.

The old couple greeted her warmly, and offered tea and biscuits, which to Penny's surprise James cheerfully accepted.

The whole interview took the best part of an hour. Mr Moore suffered from arthritis which made it difficult for him to get out, and his wife did all the shopping and gardening, as well as most of the talking. Penny was fascinated at the skilful way James asked his questions, and the genuine interest he showed in the couple's welfare.

As they stood up to leave, Penny suddenly noticed something. 'Have you hurt your leg, Mrs Moore?' she asked.

'This? Oh, it's nothing, really.' Mrs Moore pointed to a bandaged area just above her left ankle. It only just showed through her thick stockings. 'It's just a silly sore place that's taking a long time to heal up, but I think it's beginning to get better now.' The old lady gave a little smile. Penny could tell she was the type who would not want to bother anyone unless it was a matter of life and death.

'Would you like me to have a quick look at it?' she asked, trying to make the request sound conversational. 'While I'm here, I could see if there's anything we could give you to help it heal more quickly. . .'

Mrs Moore didn't look keen. 'Oh, well, if you think so, Sister. I don't want to hold you up, mind! You and Doctor, you must be so busy. . .'

'Don't worry about it, Mrs Moore,' replied James, nodding encouragement to Penny.

In her bedroom, the old lady took off her stocking, and Penny loosened the makeshift dressing. She almost gasped when she saw the deep varicose ulcer which looked as if it must have been there for a very long time.

'How long did you say you've had this sore place?'

Mrs Moore thought for a moment. 'Oh, a few weeks— a good few weeks, I suppose. I bathe it with antiseptic every day, and I *think* it's beginning to heal up, Sister. Do you know what it is?'

'It's an ulcer caused by the circulation in your leg not being very good. Antiseptic isn't really enough—we need to put some special dressings on it, Mrs Moore,' said Penny, straightening up as James came into the room to have a look.

'Will you be able to come into the surgery and let Sister dress your leg?' asked James.

'Oh, I don't know, Doctor—how often would I have to come?' Mrs Moore looked anxiously from James to Penny and back again.

'Probably twice a week at first,' suggested Penny, 'and then when the ulcer starts to heal we could make it weekly.'

'Well, if you think it's really necessary, then I suppose I'll have to. I'm coming to market tomorrow—shall I come in then?'

Back in the car, James turned and smiled at her for the first time that day. 'Well done, Penny! I must confess I didn't spot that bandage!'

'Well, neither did I until the last minute. She was very reluctant to let me see it, wasn't she?'

'That's what I mean about having to pick things up indirectly. Anyway, you did a good job.'

'Thanks!' Penny grinned, and then, remembering the

mood in which they had parted the previous evening, lapsed into silence. She gazed out of the window as they drove, admiring the little stone cottages with their mossy tiled roofs and carefully tended gardens.

James cleared his throat. 'Penny——' He paused, and she turned to look at him. He was staring at the road ahead, his jaw set in a tense line. 'Penny, I think we should clear the air, don't you?'

'What do you mean?' She knew only too well, but she was determined to make him sweat a little.

'I mean we didn't part on the best of terms last night. We've got to work together, and I'm sure we can do so perfectly amicably if we can put aside our *personal*— differences.'

'You mean confine ourselves to a working relationship? What an excellent idea!' Penny's voice was crisp, belying the little tremor she felt inside.

'Right,' said James slowly. 'Shall we consider this to be a fresh start, then?'

She nodded. 'That's fine by me.'

The next call was uneventful, and in less than an hour they were back in the practice, with just time to grab a cup of tea before launching into afternoon surgery. James seemed much less tense, and had even cracked a couple of jokes on the drive back, but it was his offer to make the tea which had everyone in the practice wondering just what had come over the man.

Friday, true to Angela's prediction, was hectic. The waiting-room almost overflowed at the beginning of morning surgery, and it was lunchtime before Penny had dealt with all her patients. Mrs Moore was one of the last to arrive, and Penny took a long time cleaning and dressing her leg ulcer, and applying a compression bandage. 'Rest your leg as much as you can,' she advised.

'I know it's difficult when you've got your husband to look after, but you've got to care for yourself as well.'

'I know—it was a surprise to find that I was the one who had to come in and have treatment,' said Mrs Moore. 'It's always been my husband who's needed to see doctors and specialists and whatnot, and I've been the fit one!'

'I think you're still pretty fit, on the whole, but you'll have to look after this leg. Keep it up on a chair when you're sitting down, and keep this dressing on until I see it again on Tuesday.'

'Thank you, Sister. You've been ever so kind. Actually, to tell you the truth, I was beginning to get a bit worried about this leg. It seemed to be taking such a long time to get better, but I didn't like to worry the doctor with it. He's always so busy, and I don't like to be a bother!'

'Dr Yorke's always got time to look at anything which is worrying you, Mrs Moore,' Penny assured her. 'He's never going to think you're being a nuisance.'

'No, I know that really. He's such a kind doctor— he's done wonders for George. We were with Dr Westlake's father for years, and then when he died, we weren't sure we'd like a young doctor, but I must say Dr Yorke is really on the ball. He got George his operation last year, and he's walking so much better now!'

As she ushered Mrs Moore out to make her next appointment, Penny mused over the fact that all James's patients seemed devoted to him. Gran had been right— he had earned the respect of this community in a very short time. Perhaps it was just as well that she wouldn't be staying long—she mustn't give him time to cast his spell over her too. Especially now that he had made it plain that she was of no interest to him except in her professional role.

It was James's half-day, so with only Neil taking afternoon surgery, things were not too hectic for Penny, and for once she was able to get away on time. She was tired, physically and mentally. The week had passed quickly, but a new job, with new skills to learn, was always exhausting at first.

She allowed herself a really lazy weekend, staying in bed until mid-morning on Saturday, which was something she had not done for a very long time. Margaret Lambert was only too pleased to leave her granddaughter to sleep for as long as she wanted—the dark shadows under Penny's eyes this week had worried her.

Monday rolled around all too soon, and Penny was back in the thick of blood tests, tetanus jabs and baby immunisations. Halfway through the morning James popped his head round the door, and Penny, remembering Jan's teasing, wondered if he was fishing for a cup of coffee, but as he advanced into the room she saw that he was carrying his bag.

'I'm just going out on a call,' he explained, 'but I thought I'd better mention that we've booked in a well woman clinic tomorrow afternoon. We'll run it together—OK?'

He was gone before Penny had a chance to say whether she thought it was OK or not—not that she had any choice in the matter. At least she wasn't expected to deal with it on her own.

The clinic was due to start at two o'clock. James suggested that they eat lunch together so that he could go through some of the basic procedures with her, and she could become familiar with the inevitable paperwork.

'We send out letters inviting all our female patients to attend the clinic, and we encourage the reluctant ones to keep their appointments!' James told her.

'What do you do if the women absolutely refuse to

attend?' Penny knew that many women were very scared
of being examined.

'Obviously we can't force people to come, but education plays a very big part. Every time I see a woman in
my surgery, I check whether she's had a cervical smear
in the last five years. If not, I explain to her why it's so
important to have a regular test, and encourage her to
make an appointment. You should be doing the same,
especially with the patients who are coming directly to
you without seeing Neil or myself.'

'Oh, dear, I haven't thought to check!' Penny bit her
lip.

'Don't worry—you can't be perfect all at once!' teased
James, smiling at her. 'You're doing fine! You've been
dumped right in at the deep end, and you're still
afloat. . .'

'Yes, I suppose so,' admitted Penny with a reluctant
smile. She looked at her watch. 'Ten minutes to go—I'd
better get the treatment-room ready. . .'

There were eight women booked in for the clinic that
afternoon, but James had warned her that she would be
lucky if five turned up. Penny saw each patient first,
asked a few questions about their general health, and
checked their weight and blood-pressure. She chatted to
them about regularly examining their own breasts for
lumps, and taught them how to do it properly. Finally,
James came in to take the cervical smear, teaching Penny
at the same time, so that when she felt confident she
could also take over this part of the procedure.

James had a real talent for helping the women to relax,
and his gentle touch, combined with constant expla-
nations of what he was doing, led to one woman after
another sitting up and saying 'That wasn't as bad as I
expected!' By the time the fifth patient had made almost
the same comment, Penny had to stop herself smiling.

She was beginning to see why so many patients expressed their admiration for 'young Dr James'. And she was having to quell a little admiration of her own.

'How about having a go on your own next week?' asked James as they packed up the slides ready to send to the laboratory. 'I'll supervise, but you can do all the work!'

'OK, I suppose I'll have to start some time!' agreed Penny. 'Do we always get such a high proportion of non-attenders?'

'I'm afraid so. Sometimes they phone to make another appointment, but usually it's a case of sending out reminders. More work for you, I'm afraid!'

The rest of the week flew past, and suddenly it was the weekend again. Halfway through her third week Penny began to feel as if she had been in the job for ages. Several of the patients who came in for regular treatment were starting to greet her like an old friend, and to her surprise she found that she was considering herself 'one of the team'. Oh, well, she told herself, enjoy it while you can. Before you know it, Jan will be wanting her job back, and you'll be out on the street.

But just a week later Penny picked up the phone to hear Steven O'Connell's anxious voice telling her that Jan had been admitted to the General Hospital with a threatened miscarriage.

'Oh, Steven——!' Penny wasn't sure what to say to comfort the poor man. 'Is there anything we can do to help?'

'Not really—there's nothing any of us can do except wait, and keep Jan's spirits up. I'm sure she'd like to see you. . .'

'Of course! I'd love to visit, but I wasn't sure. . .what about this evening?'

'She'd really appreciate it, Penny. Oh, would you give the news to Neil and James——?'

Both the doctors were very concerned to hear about Jan. 'I'm on call this evening,' said Neil, 'so I won't be able to get to the hospital until tomorrow. Will you give her my love when you see her, Penny?'

'I'd like to visit this evening,' drawled James. 'We could go at the same time, unless you'd consider that an intrusion?'

Penny sighed. Would this man never let her forget the way she had let rip at him? 'Don't be ridiculous, James,' she said wearily. 'If we're both going, we might as well go together!'

The hospital was a modern sprawl on the outskirts of town. James seemed tense on the short journey, and Penny didn't try to squeeze any conversation out of him.

Jan was sitting up in bed, with Steven at her side. She looked better than her husband, who was unshaven and bleary after spending a night and a day at the hospital. Jan greeted her visitors with a cheerful smile, but Penny could tell that her jokey exterior masked a deep concern for her unborn child.

'Now that Jan's got someone new to entertain her, I think I'll just slip home for a shave and a bite to eat,' said Steven, bending over the bed to kiss his wife tenderly.

'I've been telling him to go all day, but I couldn't get rid of him!' teased Jan. 'He just hung about like a wet weekend. Now, tell me all the news from the outside world. . .'

They stayed until the end of visiting time. Penny was amazed by Jan's apparent strength in accepting the situation. She wondered just what would have to happen to dampen this amazing woman's spirits.

'Tell Neil I'm looking forward to seeing him,' said Jan

as they took their leave. 'I do appreciate you two coming, you know.' For the first time that evening there were tears in her eyes, and she swept them away impatiently.

As they walked towards the car in the hospital car park, Penny turned to James. 'Oh, James! I feel so sorry for that couple—they want that baby so much. . .it doesn't seem fair——'

James looked down at her, his eyes tender. 'I know. That's how I feel too. Look——' he hesitated '—tell me to get lost if you like—you probably will—but what about going somewhere to cheer ourselves up? There's a jazz club that's opened recently over by the river. How would you like to try it out?'

Penny stared straight ahead, unable to answer. Memories came flooding back, stabbing at her so painfully that she almost gasped aloud. Chris had been crazy about jazz. . .

'OK—perhaps it wasn't a good idea, but there's no need to look quite so horrified!' said James ruefully.

'Oh, James, I'm sorry, I didn't mean to be rude. It's just—well, it's not my sort of thing. . .' Her voice trailed off miserably.

'Hey, what's the matter?' He looked at her in concern. 'Penny, are you all right?' He put a comforting arm around her shoulders, peering closely into her face.

Immediately she forced a smile, masking the hurt which had come so close to the surface. 'I'm fine—just a bit tired and irritable. It's been a long day.'

They drew near the car, and he released her to feel in his pockets for the keys. The brief and casual embrace had had a disquieting effect on Penny. James, on the other hand, looked as if he hadn't even been aware of touching her. She was engulfed by a sudden wave of loneliness.

They got into the car, but James didn't start the

engine immediately. Instead, he half turned in his seat
and looked intently at her again.

'There's something bothering you, isn't there?' he
asked bluntly.

Penny tried to bluff. 'I told you—Jan and Steven. . .'

'No. Something else is upsetting you—am I right?'

She gave an almost imperceptible nod.

'Would you like to talk about it?' James's voice became
gentle, persuasive. For a moment Penny was almost
tempted to pour everything out, but common sense
prevailed. For a start, she wasn't sure that he would be
very sympathetic to her story. . .

'No. Thanks for being concerned, but no, I don't
want to talk. What I want to do most of all at the
moment, actually, is eat!'

'Well, why didn't you say so?' James laughed, and
started the car with a roar.

Chinese take-away wasn't quite what she had had in
mind, but Penny had allowed herself to be persuaded.
The next question had been where to eat it. She couldn't
argue with the logic that James's cottage on the edge of
Ellminster was a lot nearer than Gran's house at Fernhill.
James dropped her off at the surgery to collect her own
car, and she followed him to a row of semi-detached
stone cottages which had once been occupied by workers
on the now disused railway.

James lived in the very last house. In the dark Penny
couldn't make out much of the surroundings, but inside
the cottage the one living-room was warm and comfortably furnished. Polished wooden stairs led up from the
corner of the room, and beyond was a tiny kitchen.

'So this is where you heat up all your take-aways?' she
teased, looking around at the modern fitted units, set out
galley-style. She had to admit, it didn't look well used.

'I'll have you know, my inability to cook is nothing but a wicked rumour! I can knock up a mean can of beans. . .'

'You'll have to get someone to teach you,' said Penny without thinking.

'Is that an offer?'

She blushed, angry with herself for her foolish remark.

While they ate, the conversation inevitably centred on work, and the common ground of their time at the Royal Western.

'Did you say your brother is there at the moment?' asked Penny.

'Yes. Poor old Kit, he's going through a bad patch at the moment. I had a letter from him a few days ago—he and his wife have just split up. I don't know why, but I have my suspicions. Kit has a knack of getting himself into trouble. Well, this time I don't think I can sort his problems out for him.'

'It sounds as if the two of you are very close,' she remarked.

'Yes—he's a lot younger than I am, and I suppose I've always felt protective. But he's grown up now, and it's time he stood on his own two feet!'

'I think it's probably time I stood on mine, too,' said Penny lightly. 'Thanks for the meal, James.'

'Do you really have to go?' James's voice was low as he reached out and gently took her hand. Knowing that she should resist, she weakly allowed herself to be drawn towards him. He raised a hand and ran it through her short hair, before tracing the line of her cheek with his finger.

'What have you done to me?' he whispered hoarsely, searching her face with eyes full of tenderness. 'You've bewitched me. I've tried to resist, but I can't. . .'

His lips claimed hers, soft at first but then with

increasing hunger and passion. With a supreme effort Penny broke away for long enough to gasp, 'James! I don't really think this is a good idea. . .'

'Nor do I!' he rasped, enfolding her more closely in his arms. Helplessly she gave herself up to the sweet demands of his kisses.

Driving to work the following morning Penny had to concentrate very hard to keep her mind on the road, instead of reliving the previous evening. It had taken an enormous amount of willpower to drag herself away from James and back to her grandmother's cottage, before too much damage had been done to the future of their professional relationship. Even so, she was nervous of seeing James this morning, suspecting that he too might be regretting his impetuosity of the night before.

She was a little early, but Angela told her as she passed through reception that James was already in his room, 'in a stinking mood!' Penny's spirits plummeted.

Perhaps it was best to speak to him straight away. The worst thing they could do would be to let the memory of last night's episode smoulder while they pretended nothing had happened. Shrinking from the task ahead, she knocked at James's door and walked in.

He was sitting on the edge of the desk, the telephone receiver in his hand as he impatiently dialled a number. Seeing Penny, he waved a letter in the air, his blue eyes glittering furiously.

'Good grief! I ask you. . .' he spluttered.

'What's the matter?' she queried.

'My brother! He's only got himself involved with some silly little nurse. Now he's lost his wife and family—and for what? For the sake of a foolish girl who by all accounts led him on in the first place. . . Oh, damn! I can't get any reply from his number!' He slammed the receiver down and glared at her. 'If I could get my hands on the irresponsible little hussy. . .'

Penny's hackles rose. 'And I suppose your brother is totally blameless?'

'Of course not,' snapped James, 'but Kit's always been easily led. He's a fool, but this scheming girl must have known she'd wreck his marriage. . .'

Penny couldn't bear to listen to any more. She was shocked—shocked that James could be so partisan, and shocked, too, to realise that he could *almost* have been talking about *her*.

CHAPTER FOUR

SHAKEN, she turned to leave the room, but James had other ideas. He jumped up from the desk and in two long strides had placed himself between her and the door.

'Don't go, Penny—I shouldn't have taken my anger out on you. I was just lashing out. . .stay a minute. We need to talk. . .'

'About what?' Penny knew she was being deliberately obtuse, but she was stalling for time, wanting to hear what James had to say before she had to reveal her own feelings.

'Can't you guess? Surely you haven't forgotten last night already?' His voice was tender, and he reached out to gently touch her cheek.

She backed away, suddenly unsure of herself. 'No, but I think perhaps that's just what we should do—forget about it. It—it shouldn't have happened. We have to work together. . .'

Her voice tailed off. James was regarding her with a wry expression. 'Don't you think we're grown-up enough to cope with being attracted to one another?'

'Well, yes, of course, but. . .' Penny felt flustered, and studiously avoided looking him in the eye. She was sure he would be able to read her thoughts. 'I think it was a mistake,' she said slowly.

He pursed his lips. He was standing very close to her, and she found his physical presence almost overwhelming. 'Look at me and say that!' he ordered.

Penny raised her head, and, her chin tilted stubbornly, repeated her words.

James drew in his breath sharply. 'I don't believe you!' His eyes were narrowed as he looked down at her. 'The girl I was kissing last night didn't think it was a mistake—she seemed to feel every bit as strongly as I did.'

Suddenly his arms were around her, his hands caressing the back of her neck, travelling down her spine, sending a hot ripple of desire snaking through the entire length of her body. 'Penny,' he whispered, his breath warm against her cheek, 'don't fight it. . .'

Penny summoned every scrap of self-control she possessed. 'I'm sorry to disappoint you, but there's nothing to fight.' Roughly she pulled away from his embrace. 'Things often look different in the cold light of day, don't they?' She looked at her watch. 'I expect we've both got patients waiting.'

Silently James stood aside. Penny left the room, aware of his eyes following her, and only when she had reached the haven of her treatment-room did she notice that her hands were shaking.

Why did I do that? she asked herself. A man I find desperately attractive tells me he feels the same way, and what do I do? I tell him to get lost! I must be completely crazy!

It was difficult to concentrate that morning, but somehow she dealt efficiently with her patients, although one regular attender commented that she didn't seem her usual chirpy self.

'Out on the town last night, Sister?' he asked, with a knowing wink.

'Something like that, Mr Jenkins.' Penny forced a cheerful smile. 'Perhaps I'm getting too old for late nights!'

'Come off it, Sister! How old are you—twenty, twenty-one——?' Bob Jenkins looked her up and down and raised a quizzical eyebrow.

Penny sighed. 'Twenty-four,' she replied in a gloomy voice. 'I'll be twenty-five in two weeks. . .'

Mr Jenkins roared with laughter. 'You're not much more than a kid! Oh, dear me, if I was twenty-four again I'd be out late every night of the week, I can tell you!'

He laughed again, rolling down his sleeve and buttoning up the cuff. He was on anti-coagulant therapy to prevent his blood clotting too easily, and a regular blood test helped the doctor to regulate the dosage of the drug.

'Same again next month, Sister?' he asked.

'Yes—you'll get the result the day after tomorrow, and I'll see you again in four weeks for the next blood test.'

As she saw Mr Jenkins out of the treatment-room, Penny realised that she was talking to the patients as if she, instead of Jan, was the regular practice nurse. Perhaps she would not be here when Mr Jenkins came back for his next blood test. The thought of having to leave the practice and all the patients she was beginning to know sent a shiver of disquiet through her.

The door opened and Neil stuck his head into the room. 'How did it go last night?' he asked.

Penny was taken aback—how could he possibly know . . .oh, of course! Jan. For one foolish moment she had assumed he was talking about herself and James.

'Jan was pretty depressed, but hiding it well,' she said, as Neil advanced into the room. 'She's such an amazing girl. We gave her your best wishes, and she said she's looking forward to seeing you.'

Neil looked pleased. 'I'll visit this afternoon—it's my half-day. Poor old Jan!' He glanced shyly at Penny. 'Did you know that she and I used to be rather close? We

went out together for quite a while—many years ago—
but it didn't work out. I think she found me too staid!'
He grinned. 'Jan's always had a bit of a wild streak in
her. Then she met Steven. . .and that was that.'

'When did you start working together?' Penny's curi-
osity was fired.

'Only a couple of years ago. We were both married by
then—which was just as well. I don't think we could
have worked under the same roof if we'd still been—you
know—*emotionally involved.*'

'No,' said Penny thoughtfully, 'I suppose that would
have been difficult. . .'

'Not just difficult, Penny—impossible! If you're too
close to someone you can't be objective—and in this job
it's essential that we can cast a critical eye over each
other's performance. The patients have got to come
first—not personal loyalties.'

'Yes, I can see that.' Penny nodded, her expression
serious.

Neil suddenly smiled. 'I'm sorry, Penny—I'm getting
on my hobbyhorse again! I'll leave you in peace. . .'

'Give my love to Jan,' she called after him. 'Tell her
I'll pop in again.'

Neil waved a hand in acknowledgement, and headed
back to his room.

Penny was in a very low mood by the time she arrived
back at Marsh Farm Cottage that evening. James, she
was convinced, had been avoiding her all day, and on
the couple of occasions when they had happened to cross
paths in the surgery he had glared at her so coldly that
her heart had seemed to freeze.

Things hadn't been helped when she had called him
in to see a patient during the afternoon. Patrick Dobson
was a balding, middle-aged man with more than a hint
of a paunch, who had asked to see the sister because he

wasn't sure whether the pains in his leg were serious enough to bother the doctor with.

'There was obviously nothing the matter with the man,' hissed James when the patient had departed. 'All he wanted was a bit of attention!'

'If someone comes in here complaining of pain, then I think they should see a doctor!' retorted Penny.

'If you'd looked at his notes properly, you'd have seen that Mr Dobson is here every five minutes. He's had pains in every imaginable place—and I've yet to find anything wrong with him!'

Penny was not going to be browbeaten. 'Well, that's your problem! If I'd sent that man home with a pat on the head, and he'd developed a deep vein thrombosis, who would be to blame? I'm a professional practitioner, James, and as such I'm accountable for my actions. Don't ask me to make judgements I'm not trained to make—it's not fair on the patients, or on me!'

'I haven't got time to stand here and listen to you spouting your "code of conduct" stuff, Penny. I've got a waiting-room full of patients. Just try to avoid calling me in to see someone who clearly isn't an urgent case. He could have been seen as an extra at the end of the list.'

This last remark made Penny feel very small. He was right—she should have asked Mr Dobson to wait until the end of surgery, instead of calling James in to see him there and then. With a sigh, she reminded herself that she was new at this job—she still had a lot to learn, and unfortunately most of her mistakes were likely to be picked up by James. The only good thing to come out of the episode was a strengthening of her belief that to start a relationship with him would be a terrible mistake.

She was turning all this over in her mind while she sat with her grandmother that evening, watching a film on television. Penny's eyes were on the screen, but her

thoughts were elsewhere. Over and over again she tried
to make some sort of sense out of the events of the past
two days. When Margaret Lambert got up stiffly from
the sofa and turned off the television, Penny realised
with surprise that the film had ended without her even
noticing.

'Is something bothering you, darling? Is it the job?'
The old lady peered at her granddaughter with tender
concern.

'No—well, yes, I suppose it is. I just think I'm
beginning to settle into it, and then something happens
to make me realise that I'm not as clever as I thought I
was. And it's usually something pretty stupid—something I should have known!'

Margaret Lambert smiled. 'And I suppose you don't
get much sympathy from the doctors?'

'None at all from James Yorke! And he always seems
to be the one to see me mess things up!' sighed Penny.

'Does that bother you?' asked her grandmother. 'Do
you want him to have a good opinion of you?'

'As a nurse, yes!' Penny's eyes blazed. 'I don't care
what he thinks of me personally, but I'm damned if I'm
going to let him think I'm useless at my job!'

Mrs Lambert watched her thoughtfully. 'I had an idea
that you two might be getting along quite well—after
all, you were out together until very late last night. . .'

'Sorry, Gran, don't get your hopes up. I've seen a side
of James Yorke today that I neither expected nor liked.
You can carry on thinking he's Dr Wonderful, but I'm
afraid I don't share your admiration!'

'Hmm. Pity. . .' Margaret gave her granddaughter a
comforting pat on the shoulder.

The weekend came as a welcome relief for Penny. On
Saturday afternoon Margaret was preparing to stroll

down to the village to help with the Women's Institute jumble sale, an event she hated to miss because everyone in Fernhill would be there, young and old. 'What are you going to do, dear?' she asked. 'Are you coming down to the church hall?'

Penny pulled a face. 'I think I'll give it a miss, Gran. Jumble sales aren't really my sort of thing—they always make me feel rather sad. All those unwanted possessions! I think I'll go into town and do a bit of shopping—I might call in at the hospital and see Jan for a few minutes.'

'Good idea—there are one or two things you can get for me, if you wouldn't mind. . .'

Armed with a list, Penny set off in her Mini and spent an enjoyable afternoon strolling around the town. With her shopping complete, she drove to the hospital. Jan might already have visitors, of course, in which case Penny planned to leave the magazines she had brought and come straight home.

To her surprise, she found Jan alone. She lay against the pillows, her face pale, her eyes closed, listening to a music cassette through a pair of headphones.

Gently Penny touched her shoulder. Instantly Jan's eyes flew open, and after a moment's surprise she greeted Penny with a huge smile.

'How super to see you!' she cried, wrenching off the headphones and returning Penny's kiss. 'Steven's gone to fetch his mum and dad—they'll be here a bit later. Oh, I can't tell you how bored I'm getting, lying here day after day!'

They chattered on for a while. Jan wanted to know everything that Penny had been doing at work, and Penny for her part was only too pleased to ask for Jan's advice. Once they had dealt with the nursing problems, Jan turned her attention to the practice staff.

'I hope James hasn't got you making his coffee, Penny,' she said with a smile.

Penny rolled her eyes. 'He'd be lucky! I'm afraid James and I are not actually on the best of terms at the moment.'

Jan sat up, agog at the whiff of some interesting gossip. 'Come on, tell your Auntie Jan all about it!'

Penny sighed. 'There's not a great deal to tell. James is a bad-tempered, chauvinistic beast!'

'Is that all?' laughed Jan.

'He's so changeable, Jan. I don't know what to make of him. One moment he's so. . .*charming*, and the next he's ranting and raving at me about his brother as if it was my fault!'

'You've lost me—as if what was your fault?' queried Jan.

'Apparently his brother has had an affair with a nurse in London, and now his marriage has broken up.'

'Oh, dear, that won't please James at all,' said Jan with a long face. 'Whoever finally reaches the altar with that man needn't worry about him straying away from home—our James has very old-fashioned ideas about marriage!'

'How do you know?' asked Penny, intrigued.

Jan merely gave a knowing wink. 'So, why did you come in for the rough end of James's temper?'

'Because I happened to be standing in the firing line. Also, his brother works at my old hospital—perhaps I seem to be a link.'

'That's a coincidence—do you know him?'

Penny shook her head. 'I've been racking my brains to try and remember anyone of that name, but it doesn't ring a bell. I'd probably know him by sight. . .'

'I bet James blamed the girl more than his brother, didn't he?' asked Jan shrewdly.

'You've got it! According to him, she's a scheming little hussy, a marriage-wrecker. Not that he knows the first thing about her. . .'

'What a shame I'm missing all this drama!' sighed Jan wistfully.

Penny didn't seem to hear. 'After all,' she carried on heatedly, 'James has no idea whether this girl was even aware that his brother was married! She might have become involved quite innocently. It does happen——!'

'Does it?' Jan looked at her curiously. 'You sound as if you're speaking from first-hand experience!'

Penny's first instinct was to deny it, hide her secret away as she had for so long, but suddenly she was overcome with a desire to talk to someone.

'Jan, can I confide in you?' she asked. 'I mean, *really* confide—I don't want this to get back to anyone in the practice. . .'

Jan's expression became serious. 'Of course. I'd never betray your trust, Penny.'

Penny paused for a moment, wondering where to start. 'You're right, I am speaking from experience. I was staffing at the Royal Western, and I met a doctor at a party. . .we hit it off right away. Chris was so different from anyone I'd dated before. He was a surgical SHO, and I was on the medical unit, so we didn't see much of each other at work. I suppose he seemed different because he kept away from the medical scene. He took me to jazz clubs, and theatres, and even whisked me off to the south of France for a holiday. . .' Her voice trailed off as she relived her memories.

'What went wrong?' prompted Jan.

'I went to lunch in the canteen one day, and Chris was a few places ahead of me in the queue. He was talking to another doctor, and I heard him ask, "How's your wife,

Chris?" And Chris replied, "She's very well. The baby's due in a couple of months".'

There was silence for a moment while both women thought this over. Finally Jan spoke. 'And that was how you found out that he was married?'

Penny nodded. 'I couldn't believe my ears. I thought it must be some sort of joke—but of course it wasn't. Suddenly things began to make sense—I'd never seen where he lived. He always told me he was ashamed of the grotty flat he shared with other doctors, but obviously that was a lie. One of many.'

'So what happened?'

'I confronted him, and told him I didn't want to see him again. He cried. It was terrible, and it got worse. He began to pester me, turning up on the ward and ringing me up all the time. It almost seemed like an obsession. People at the hospital began to realise that we'd been having an affair, and so the gossip started. You can imagine—he was a married man with a pregnant wife, so I was the "other woman". People I'd known for years began to cut me dead.'

'Oh, Penny, how awful!' Jan's voice was full of sympathy. 'What did you do about it?'

'I gave in. I couldn't stand it in the end—I handed in my notice and left London.'

'What happened to the doctor?'

'No idea. He doesn't know where to find me, thank goodness.' Penny sighed. 'So that's why I was shocked when James jumped to so many conclusions. Listen, Jan——' she took hold of her friend's hand and looked earnestly into her face '—please promise me you won't breathe a word of this to anyone—especially not James.'

'Of course I promise. But I think you're misjudging him, Penny. If he heard your story I'm sure he'd understand. . .'

'I don't intend to find out. He's not going to hear it.'

'Perhaps he'll have to, one day.'

'What do you mean?' asked Penny.

Jan looked thoughtful. 'I think our Dr Yorke is rather attracted to you,' she said.

Penny tried to look unconcerned, doggedly pushing away the memory of James's arms around her, his mouth on hers. . . 'I hardly think that's likely,' she lied.

'Penny, I've known James for quite a while now, and I've noticed the way he looks at you. I've never seen that expression in his eyes before. And I suspect you're not as indifferent as you make out—am I right?'

A sudden blush gave Penny away, and she ran her hands despairingly through her hair. 'OK, so maybe I find him attractive—perhaps it's mutual. But after Chris—well, let's just say it'll be a very long time before I trust my heart to another man!'

'Cricket on the green—this takes me right back to my childhood!' commented Penny the following afternoon.

'Yes—do you remember how you used to sit with Grandpa when he did the scoring?' asked Margaret.

'Those summers seemed idyllic. In my memory it was always sunny—but I suppose it did rain sometimes?'

Margaret laughed. 'Of course—a lot! Now of course, in *my* childhood it *never* rained in the summer!'

'Has Fernhill got a good team these days?' asked Penny as they strolled slowly up the lane to the village green.

'I'm not sure who'll be playing this year—this is the first match of the season. Some of the old regulars are getting a bit long in the tooth, but I dare say there'll be some new young blood. Oh, look, there's Daphne! Let's go and sit with her—I want to ask her about her son. . .'

Penny sat down with the two old ladies and pretended

to watch the game. She wasn't really very keen on cricket—despite her grandfather's best efforts, she had never quite managed to grasp the finer points of scoring. But on a pleasant day in late April with the sun warm on her face, she was quite content to sit in a deck-chair in the open air and enjoy the atmosphere. She looked around with interest at the other spectators. Most of the villagers seemed to have turned out for this opening match, encouraged by the sunshine. At the back of the pavilion a growing knot of children played noisily. Idly Penny turned her attention to the cricket.

Suddenly she sat forward and peered across the cricket pitch. Surely—surely the batsman at the far end, immaculate in his whites, was James Yorke?

She turned to her grandmother, who was watching her with an amused expression.

'I wondered how long it would take you to notice young James,' she said with a knowing smile.

'Good grief,' muttered Penny. 'The man gets everywhere! What on earth is he doing playing for Fernhill—he doesn't even live in the village?'

'If the cricket club had to rely on recruiting from the village alone, I doubt if they'd ever make up a team.' Margaret nodded towards James, who was just making a run. 'I've heard he's a very good batsman.'

At that moment the little crowd of spectators gave a cry of disappointment, as James was run out. With a cheerful shrug he strolled off the pitch and into the pavilion.

'I obviously spoke too soon. Why don't you go and offer your condolences?' suggested Margaret.

'Gran, you must be joking!' retorted Penny, and firmly planting her sunglasses on her nose, turned her attention once more to the action on the pitch.

The afternoon crept past, and she began to find the

gentle murmuring of the spectators and the thwack of the bat against the ball soporific. She leaned back in her deck-chair and closed her eyes.

When she opened them again it took her a few moments to notice the two long white-flannelled legs stretched out in the chair beside her. Startled, she turned her head to find James watching her intently.

She was glad of her dark glasses. She didn't want James to see how his presence flustered her.

'Hello—I must have been asleep,' she said. 'Have you been there long?'

'A few minutes. You looked so peaceful, it seemed a shame to wake you up!'

Penny looked around. 'Where did Gran go?'

'She's in the pavilion, helping with the tea. This is our last batsman.' He nodded towards the pitch.

'How many runs did you get?'

'Seven.' James pulled a face. 'Not a very good performance for the opening match of the season—I blame it on you.'

Penny sat up straight, wrenching off her sunglasses to glare angrily at him. 'Whatever is that supposed to mean?'

He laughed. 'Whoa, calm down, spitfire! I only meant that your presence was a distraction. Once I'd noticed you sitting there, I couldn't keep my mind on the game. . .' His blue eyes twinkled. 'Instead of watching that hulking great bowler, I found myself looking at you—a far more appealing sight, I must say!'

He looked approvingly at her stone-coloured trousers and the exotically patterned loose cotton sweater which contrasted well with her fair hair and creamy skin. Penny knew the outfit suited her, but James's frankly appraising look was disquieting, and she hid once again behind her dark glasses.

Out of the corner of her eye she noticed her grandmother hurry out of the pavilion, waving agitatedly in her direction. 'Whatever's wrong with Gran?' Penny jumped up from her seat. 'Something's happened!'

She hurried across the grass towards the pavilion, with James at her heels. Margaret Lambert met them at the door, her face ashen. 'It's Daphne,' she gasped, 'she dropped the bread knife and she's cut herself very badly. . .'

Margaret's friend was sitting in the middle of a little huddle of women, clutching a blood-stained tea-towel to her leg.

'May we see, Daphne?' asked Penny gently. Carefully she removed the cloth to reveal a long gaping gash.

'It was so silly—I don't know how it happened. . .' cried Daphne. 'The knife just seemed to slip from my hand, and the next moment——'

'Don't worry—it's not too bad,' said Penny, watching as James took a look at the wound.

'I'm afraid it's going to need a few stitches,' he said, straightening up. 'I'll get some dressings from my car, but I can't suture it for you here—it'll mean a trip to Casualty.'

Penny knew that Daphne lived alone. 'I'll drive you to the hospital,' she said straight away.

'Oh, Penny dear, you're so kind!' The elderly lady smiled apologetically. 'I'm sorry to be such a bother. . .'

'You're not a bother. Let's just hope you won't have to hang around for too long before they can get that leg stitched up.'

James returned from his car with a handful of dressing packs and a bandage, and swiftly Penny padded the wound with a sterile dressing and bandaged it firmly.

Five minutes later Penny had fetched her car and they were on their way to the hospital. Casualty was moderately busy, and by the time they had waited to be seen by a doctor, and waited again to be stitched up by the charge nurse, two hours had gone by.

'What a terrible waste of your Sunday afternoon, Penny,' moaned Daphne on the way home.

'Don't give it another thought. I'm just glad the damage wasn't more serious.'

They arrived at Daphne's house, and Penny helped her in and made sure she was comfortable before she drove on past the village green, where the last stragglers of the cricket game were leaving the pavilion.

As she drew up outside Marsh Farm Cottage she noticed James's car pull in behind her.

'How did you get on?' he asked, leaning his arms across the top of the open driver's door. He looked fit and relaxed in jeans and a rugby shirt.

Penny locked her car and strolled over to join him. 'Fine. We had a bit of a wait, but Daphne was in good spirits when I left her.'

'I'm sure it wasn't quite the way you intended to spend your Sunday afternoon,' mused James.

'Oh, I didn't mind. I seem to be seeing a lot of Ellminster General Hospital at the moment!'

'Yes—I popped in to see Jan last night. She mentioned that you'd been in earlier.'

Penny looked sharply at James. Surely Jan wouldn't have broken her promise and repeated anything to James? No, that was silly. He looked quite unconcerned.

'I didn't get a chance to ask you on Friday,' he said, watching her closely, 'but there's a one-day seminar coming up in a couple of weeks on diabetic care in the community. If you'd be interested in going, let me know. The practice will pay the fee. Think about it and let me know at work tomorrow.'

He climbed back into his car and with a brisk wave was gone.

CHAPTER FIVE

THE details were on her desk when Penny arrived at work the following morning. She read the leaflet avidly. The seminar was to be held in a hotel in Bath, and was open to all community nurses, practice nurses and general practitioners involved in the care of diabetic patients. The fee for the day sounded astronomical, and Penny was relieved to know that she wouldn't be expected to pay out of her own pocket.

She caught James just as he was leaving for his rounds. 'I'd like to attend that seminar, if places are still available,' she said.

He smiled and nodded. 'Good—I thought you'd be interested. I'll ask Joan to send off your fee this afternoon.'

Over the next few days Penny read up as much as she could on recent research into diabetes. The programme of lectures and discussions sounded very high-powered, and she didn't want to be left floundering.

The seminar was scheduled for a Friday—Penny's birthday—and at the beginning of that week she decided to remind Neil that he and James would be without a nurse that day.

'I shouldn't worry—there won't be many patients in, and I can deal with any odd bits and pieces which might turn up.' Neil gave a cheerful shrug.

Penny frowned. 'Why aren't you expecting many patients?' she asked.

'Because I'll be on my own,' replied Neil, giving her a puzzled look. 'I'm not getting a locum in!'

'But where will James be?'

'He's going to the seminar with you—didn't you know?' Neil looked surprised.

Penny pursed her lips. 'No. No, I didn't. James seems to have forgotten to mention that little detail. . .'

She cornered him in his room a few minutes before afternoon surgery.

'Why didn't you tell me you're going to the seminar?' she demanded.

He looked up, surprised at her tone. 'I assumed you knew.'

'Well, you assumed wrong!' cried Penny hotly.

'Does it make a difference?' asked James, his voice smooth. 'I'm not really sure what it is you're so upset about! It seems a simple enough thing. . .'

She frowned. 'If you're going to Bath, then I'm staying here!'

His eyes surveyed her coldly. 'What will you tell Neil—that you can't go to the seminar because you can't bear to spend a few hours in a lecture hall with James Yorke and a hundred other people?'

Penny realised she was running the risk of sounding extremely foolish. But how could she explain to James that she needed to keep her distance from him—that she didn't trust herself to spend too long in his company?

'I can assure you,' he continued, 'that I had no ulterior motive in suggesting that you came to the seminar. I just thought it would be educational for both of us, and beneficial for our patients in the long run. I'm not planning any extra-curricular activities, if that's what you're worried about. . .'

'I didn't think—I mean, I'm not. . .' Penny bit her lip. 'I'm over-reacting, aren't I?' she asked sheepishly, and raising her eyes to look at him, found him watching her with a definite gleam of amusement.

'Just a little,' he agreed, smiling.

'Is it too late to ask for a lift to Bath?' she asked cheekily.

It was a demanding day. The lectures began at nine sharp, and continued throughout the day, with breaks for coffee and tea, and an excellent lunch. During the drive down to Bath the conversation had centred on medical matters and Penny was grateful for that. It removed the need to worry about her feelings for James.

She had been nervous walking into the conference room, which was packed with people who seemed to know each other and were all talking animatedly. James apparently sensed her trepidation, and took her firmly by the arm. Together they collected their programmes for the day, and were ushered on to be given a welcome cup of coffee. James spotted a few faces he knew, and dutifully introduced Penny, but after polite greetings the doctors quickly forgot to include her in their conversation, and she was left looking around for a friendly face.

She detached herself from the group of GPs and approached a trio of women who looked about as lost as she was. They chatted for a while about their respective surgeries, then drifted over to look at the medical trade stands which were promoting their products. Penny learned that as well as giving her a chance to talk to the reps, this was the place to pick up free handouts of rubber gloves, paper tissues and notepads for her treatment-room.

The first lecture was announced, and everyone hurried to take their seats. Penny looked around, wondering where to go and who to sit with. A hand seized her elbow.

'I've reserved a place for you!' James's voice in her ear

was, for once, very welcome, and she allowed herself to be propelled across the room to where two chairs remained empty at the end of a row.

'This chap's the leading diabetic specialist in this part of the country,' James whispered, as the consultant began his talk.

Soon Penny was completely absorbed in the subject, no longer aware of James's presence beside her. She took notes, and enjoyed the intelligent questions which were put forward at the end of the lecture. A heated discussion on the relative merits of community-based versus hospital-based diabetic care spilled over from the end of the lecture right through the ten-minute coffee break.

At lunchtime James turned to Penny and smiled apologetically.

'Do you mind if I abandon you for lunch? I've got one or two things to see to—will you be all right on your own?'

She bristled. 'I think I might just about manage to survive an hour without you, James.' She tried to sound light-hearted, but the barb in her words was not lost on him.

'Sorry, I did sound patronising, didn't I? Enjoy your lunch!'

Penny managed to meet up with the three nurses she had met earlier, and they sat at a table together.

'Who was that dishy man you were with?' asked one, looking around. 'What have you done with him?'

She pulled a face. 'That's one of the partners in my practice. He's not having lunch—he disappeared off somewhere.'

'Pity. I was hoping for an introduction. . .is he married?' asked the girl, while her friends laughed and groaned.

With the ice well and truly broken, lunch became a

very noisy and enjoyable affair, and by the time they headed off towards another, smaller conference-room for a practice nurse 'workshop' Penny hadn't given James or his disappearance another thought.

They joined up again with the GPs for the final session of the day, and she immediately noticed James's dark head bowed in conversation with the man on his right. She was about to take a seat with her new friends, but suddenly James turned to search the faces around him, and, spotting Penny, he raised his hand and pointed to an empty seat beside him.

She was about to ignore this gesture, but her companions had other ideas. 'Go on, girl! If you're not interested, there are plenty here who are! Go on, Penny. . .' Several hands shoved her towards the waiting chair.

Embarrassed, she tried to slip into the seat without attracting the attention of James, who was once again talking earnestly to his neighbour.

For a moment or two she sat organising her sheaf of notes ready for the lecture. She realised that James had stopped talking and was watching her silently.

'Hi. Good lunch?' he smiled.

She nodded, trying to pretend to herself that her heart was not racing at the sight of his smile.

The speaker stepped up to the lectern. James leaned close and whispered in her ear.

'Do you like Shakespeare? *Twelfth Night?*'

Penny frowned, wondering whether he had gone a little mad. Why was he sitting in a medical lecture, asking her about Shakespeare?

'Yes, it's one of my favourite plays. I studied it at school.'

'Good.' James looked pleased. 'I just happen to have two tickets to the theatre in Bath this evening.'

'What the hell are you playing at?' hissed Penny in his ear, as the eminent consultant in front of them began to deliver his speech on the prevention and management of diabetic retinopathy.

James merely grinned, and settled down to listen to the lecture.

Penny found it hard to concentrate at first, as her irritation with him smouldered away, but before long she was absorbed in the subject and her annoyance was forgotten.

The day ended with a question-and-answer session which was so enthusiastic that many people had no chance to air their views. A vote of thanks to the speakers was followed by a spontaneous round of applause. Penny rose to leave feeling the warm satisfaction of a day well spent.

A hand on her shoulder reminded her that in James's opinion the day was not yet over.

'Well——?' He gently turned her so that she was facing him. Looking earnestly into her eyes, he continued, 'How about a spot of culture? It seems a pity to waste those tickets.'

Penny shook her head in exasperation. 'You're very confident, James. What makes you think I haven't got plans for this evening?'

He grinned broadly. 'I've done a little detective work. My spies tell me that you were planning a long hot bath and a cup of cocoa—now don't you think dinner and the theatre sounds rather more appealing?'

'You're impossible!'

'I know. Come on, let's get out of here and find somewhere to eat.'

Sitting opposite James in a busy wine bar near the theatre, Penny suddenly clapped a hand to her face.

'Gran! I nearly forgot—I'd better ring her and tell her not to expect me. . .'

'No need.' James shook his head. 'It's all taken care of. Happy birthday!' He raised his wine glass in a toast.

The colour flooded her cheeks, and she laughed self-consciously. 'You rat! Do you mean Gran was in on all this?'

'I told you I'd been playing detective. I happened to ask your grandmother if she knew whether you had plans for this evening. I had no idea it was your birthday until then. Margaret was very disappointed that you seemed intent on celebrating with hot chocolate and a good book!'

'Oh, no!' Penny rolled her eyes. 'There'll be no holding Gran now that she knows we're spending the evening together—she'll be impossible to live with!'

'You mean she's already decided that we're right for each other?'

Penny nodded, smiling ruefully.

'Well, I'm glad someone shares my opinion!'

They emerged from the theatre in a buoyant mood, the beauty of the Shakespearian language still ringing in their ears. Penny was too tired, and too content, to object when James's arm snaked around her shoulders as they strolled through the streets towards the car park. It felt so right as they walked in step, her body fitting snugly against his. She could feel the hard muscles of his thighs as his leg brushed hers, and she felt a sudden surge of desire. He seemed so strong—so alive! Seeming to sense her thoughts, James's tightened his arm around her and they continued in companionable silence.

With the car in sight, he looked down fondly at her. 'Was it a better way of spending your birthday than with your cocoa?' he asked.

'Oh, yes! The play was wonderful—wonderful! I can't thank you enough, James. . .'

They stopped, and she looked up at him, her eyes shining, the unexpected pleasure of the evening enveloping her like a warm cloak.

He bent down to wrap her in his arms. His lips brushed hers in a feather-light kiss, and he drew back slightly to search her face with hungry eyes. Penny, aware that she was walking a dangerous path, tilted her face to his, and gave herself up to his demanding kisses.

At last he released her a little, and groaned in mock despair. 'Penny, what are you doing to me? Here I am, a respectable country GP, kissing a beautiful woman in the street. . .'

'Are you accusing me of sullying your whiter-than-white reputation?' she asked with a cheeky grin.

'I'd be only too pleased to have my reputation sullied by you, you little imp!' James gave her chin a playful tweak and drew her to his side to resume their journey to the car. Shopping streets led off to their right, but on the other side was a crescent of Georgian town houses, some of them now converted into smart hotels with softly lit windows.

'It's very late,' he commented, 'and it's a long way to Ellminster. We don't *have* to go home tonight. . .'

'Yes, we do,' said Penny firmly. 'Don't forget, I've got a hot bath and cocoa waiting for me at home.'

James squeezed her a little tighter. 'I'm sure we could find somewhere to stay with plenty of hot water. . .'

'No, James. It's been a great evening—let's just take one step at a time. There's no hurry.'

Shrugging his acceptance, he unlocked the car and held open the door for her. They drove out of the city. The car was warm, and music played softly. Penny's eyes began to close. . .

'Penny——' James's voice was deep and serious, and instantly she was wide awake. 'I think you must realise by now how I feel about you—I know I'm pretty useless at hiding things! You've come to mean something very special to me. You'd better tell me now if I'm wasting my time, before I make an even bigger fool of myself!'

His eyes were fixed firmly on the road ahead. Penny took a deep breath, wondering how to answer. She didn't want him to know just how much she returned his feelings—after all, how did she know he was telling the truth? Other men lied—why should James Yorke be any different? On the other hand, if she rejected him now, she might lose him forever. . .

'Well?' At last he flicked his glance in her direction, and she could see that beneath his flippant exterior he was anxious. He had laid his cards on the table—now it was her turn.

'I—I can't deny that I feel something for you, James,' she began, deciding that perhaps honesty was the best path to take, 'but I'm scared. I've been hurt badly before, and I'm not sure I'm ready to risk that kind of pain again.'

Instantly he reached out a hand and found hers, squeezing it tightly before taking the steering wheel again. 'Want to tell me about it?' he asked gently.

'No, not yet——'

'So where do we go from here, Penny?'

'I think—we could get to know each other a little better. . .see how things go. . .'

James smiled. That sounds very sedate. Sedate but with a hint of promise.'

Penny laughed. 'That's my best offer,' she teased.

'Then I suppose I'll just have to settle for it,' he growled.

They drove on in a relaxed silence. After a while

Penny dozed again, only waking when the car drew up outside Marsh Farm Cottage.

James stilled the engine. 'So,' he whispered into the darkness, 'does this sedate, "getting to know each other" include a goodnight kiss?'

'I'd be very disappointed if it didn't,' Penny smiled.

He cupped her face in his hands and gently kissed her forehead, her eyelids, the tip of her nose, and at last brushed his lips tantalisingly over her mouth. 'How could anyone hurt you, Penny?' he whispered. 'I'd like to string up the man who caused you pain. . .'

'Ssh! That's in the past—I'm here with you now. . .' This time the kiss was deep and lingering, and as Penny let her fingertips explore the back of James's neck, the breadth of his shoulders, she marvelled over the effect this man's kisses had on her whole being.

At last they drew apart. 'I suppose I'd better go in. . .' she sighed.

'I know. You've got your bath and cocoa waiting!'

She giggled. 'I might forgo the cocoa—unless of course you'd like to join me?'

James groaned. 'No, thanks—intrigued as I am by your cosy bedtime rituals, I think I'd better go home to my celibate bed. . . I suppose I can't persuade you to——'

'No.' Penny's attempt to sound stern was ruined by another giggle. 'Thank you for this evening, James.' She opened the car door and climbed out. James got out as well, stepping around the front of the car to wrap her in his arms again.

'It was the least I could do on your birthday,' he whispered into her ear. 'Go in now, before I try to drag you home with me. . .'

Alone in her room, she found that her tiredness had deserted her. She sat by the window listening to the night sounds—a dog barking over on the farm, some unseen creature scuttling through the undergrowth next to the house. Oh, James, she thought, I wasn't ready for this. It's taken me by surprise—I can feel my defences crumbling. . .

CHAPTER SIX

IT WAS nearly eleven before Penny appeared downstairs the following morning. Her grandmother raised her eyebrows knowingly. 'Late night?' she asked.

Penny planted a kiss on the old lady's cheek. 'Quite late—but it took me hours to get to sleep. I know I was still awake at four—I heard the church clock chiming.'

'And how was the seminar?'

'The seminar was very interesting—very worthwhile. I learned a lot. . .and, as you well know, Grandmother dear, I was taken out to the theatre afterwards to celebrate my birthday!'

'Was that worthwhile too?' Margaret surveyed her granddaughter with a steady gaze, noting the colour rising on Penny's cheeks.

'You could say that. We had a lovely evening, Gran. The play was wonderful—I'll show you the programme.'

'So you've changed your mind about James Yorke's being arrogant and self-opinionated?'

Penny straightened her back and glared at her grandmother. 'Who said I've changed my mind? I still think he's both those things——' her expression softened and she grinned '—but he's got some good points too!'

'I'm glad you think so, because he's already been on the phone twice this morning. He was very anxious to speak to you, but when I said you were still asleep he wouldn't hear of waking you. He's ringing again later.'

'Oh. I wonder what he wants?' Penny tried to sound nonchalant, but her heart was thumping so hard she wondered whether her grandmother could hear it.

Half an hour later the telephone rang, and Penny forced herself to let it ring a few times before she picked it up.

'Hello?'

'Good morning, lazybones! You're up at last!' Penny could tell that James was smiling. She imagined his eyes, crinkled at the corners when he laughed. . .

'I'm sorry—what did you say?' she asked.

'Listen—Neil's not well, he's gone down with some bug, so I've got to be on call for the rest of the weekend. It's a damned nuisance, because I was going to suggest that we went out somewhere today, but these things happen. . .'

'That's a pity. Poor Neil.'

'Yes, he sounded pretty rough on the phone. Anyway, what I wondered was—how about keeping me company while I wait by the phone?'

'At your house? Oh, I. . .' Penny thought of the temptations of spending so much time with James, alone in his house. . .'I don't know——' she said doubtfully.

'No strings, Penny, I promise. Just company—we could cook a meal together, talk over the ideas thrown up by the seminar——'

'Cook together? Are you serious?' Penny laughed. 'James, by your own admission you can't cook! Come on, admit it—you just want me to feed you.'

'Oh, Penny!' James's disembodied voice became deep in mock indignation. 'How could you think me so mercenary? Don't you think this would be a good opportunity to start my cookery lessons?'

Penny chuckled. 'OK. I suppose you want me to shop for this meal as well?'

'How did you guess?' he laughed.

'You're a crafty old so-and-so, James Yorke! I'll see you later.'

She arrived on James's doorstep later that afternoon with a bulging bag of groceries in her arms.

'That's all for one meal?' asked James, relieving her of her burden. 'Or are you staying all week?'

'No—that's just our supper!' she retorted, flinging her jacket on to the back of an armchair and marching into the kitchen.

'Pity. . .' he murmured, creeping up softly behind her to nuzzle the back of her neck.

Penny clutched at the worktop, her knees turning to jelly. 'James—please. . .' she gasped, squirming out of his grasp. 'I don't think—I mean—let's just cook, OK?'

He groaned. 'OK, OK—I promise I'll behave myself. But it's damned hard, Penny—you don't know the effect you have on me.'

I think I can guess, mused Penny as she unpacked the ingredients she had bought to make lasagne. 'This is a good recipe to start you off on the art of cooking—and it won't spoil too much if you're called out at the last moment!'

James pulled a face. 'Yes, that's what usually happens. I've only had two calls today, but I'll lay bets that the moment we sit down to eat—bingo!'

'Never mind, let's make the best of it. Now, do you know what this is called?' She held up an onion, and dodged the playful fist aimed at her by a grinning James.

How the lasagne got as far as reaching the oven Penny never knew. She didn't think she had laughed so much in her life as she did during the preparation of that dish—and as for teaching James some basic cookery skills. . .

At last the Parmesan cheese was sprinkled on the top and the whole dish disappeared into the oven.

'Right, we leave it now for a good half-hour,' said Penny, wiping her hands on a cloth.

'Good. What shall we do to pass the time?' asked James in a wicked voice.

'Wash up the pans?' she suggested innocently.

'No.' He whipped off the tea-towel she had tucked around her waist in place of an apron, and taking her by the hand dragged her into the living-room. 'You've worked quite hard enough already. Come and sit down—I'll do the washing up later.'

He poured her a glass of red wine, and half filled a glass for himself. Raising his glass to her, he proposed a toast. 'To us. Long may our—*friendship*—continue.'

'To us,' echoed Penny quietly, sipping her wine. She leaned back in the chair, and sighed contentedly.

James sat down on the rug, his back against her chair. His long legs were stretched out, his wine glass held balanced on his knee. His dark head rested against her leg, and she had an almost overwhelming desire to run her fingers through the thick, springy hair.

Suddenly he looked up and narrowed his eyes. 'Are you happy living out here, Penny? Don't you miss London at all?'

Penny shook her head. 'No, I don't. I'm enjoying my new job—and I love the countryside around here. It's a total change—and I think that's what I needed.'

'Someone in London hurt you, didn't they—or should I say he?'

She hesitated. James was watching her intently. 'Yes,' she replied at last, tempted for a moment to pour out everything, but at the last moment her nerve let her down. 'I don't want to talk about it, James—not yet.'

'I understand.' He reached up and took her hand, holding it gently. Her small fingers were completely engulfed in his large, strong hand, and she marvelled over how such a large, powerful man could at the same time be so delicate in his touch.

The tenderness of the moment was shattered by the
shrill tones of the phone on the table by the front door.
With a sigh James jumped up from the floor and crossed
the room in a couple of long strides.

'Hello—yes?' He spoke for a few moments to the
unseen caller, who was, to judge by the calming tone of
James's voice, in a bit of a panic. 'So is she still in the
bath?' he was asking. 'Who else is there? All right, I'll
be with you in a few minutes. . .what? Oh, I see—
well. . .' He turned and looked at Penny, raising his
eyebrows slightly, 'I can bring my nurse with me if you
think. . .yes. . .goodbye.'

Putting his hands on his hips, he looked at the ceiling
and let out a long breath. 'I'm sorry about the supper,
Penny, but I've got to go out—and I think I'm going to
need your help. Come on—I'll explain on the way.'

Penny ran into the kitchen to turn the oven down
before following James, who was already out of the house
and in the car.

Driving through the town and out on to the Gloucester
road, he told her that May Soames, an elderly spinster
who lived with her sister Violet in an isolated cottage,
had been taken ill while in the bath, and it was her sister
who had rung in great distress.

'They're great characters, both of them,' James said,
'but I can't help wondering if they should be on their
own. Neither of them has been very well lately, and now
Violet can't get May out of the bath on her own. The
other problem is that they're both very, very shy—and
that's where you come in. Having another woman present is going to be a great help. May would not be happy
at being helped out of her bath by a man!'

'What do you think is wrong with her?' asked Penny.
'If she's been taken acutely ill perhaps they should have
just called an ambulance?'

'Yes, I'm inclined to agree, but knowing the Soames sisters, I suspect that the thought of a couple of burly ambulancemen appearing in their bathroom would be enough to finish off the pair of them! I suspect it's May's heart trouble again—she's suffered from left ventricular failure for some years. Violet said she was very breathless and cyanosed. Anyway, we'll soon find out. Here we are!'

In a couple of minutes they were being shown up the stairs by an anxious Violet, who appeared greatly relieved to see Penny.

'Oh, my dear—thank goodness! My sister will be so embarrassed to have to be helped like this—and the young doctor. . .oh, dear. . .!' She tailed off into a nervous silence, and Penny tried to give her a reassuring smile.

'Please don't worry, Miss Soames—I'm sure it won't take long to help your sister out of that bath and into her own bed. Is this the bathroom?'

Penny was pleased to find that the room was warm, and the old lady sitting in the now empty bath was draped around with a large blanket. As she looked more closely at the swathed figure, however, her heart sank as she realised that there was little resemblance between the two sisters. Where Violet was tiny and birdlike, smaller even than Penny herself, May was tall and solid. Pushing away her doubts as to whether they would ever manage to lift this portly woman out of the high, old-fashioned tub, Penny knelt down on the floor.

'How are you feeling, Miss Soames?' she asked, taking the woman's wrist gently between her fingers and feeling for the pulse. Looking up, May nodded breathlessly, but didn't speak. She was leaning forward over her knees, her breathing very laboured, and an unhealthy blue tinge around her lips.

'I've brought Dr Yorke to see you,' Penny said quietly but clearly. 'He's going to give you an injection to take some of the fluid off your lungs and help you breathe more easily. Your sister and I will be here with you all the time. . .'

May nodded again, but Penny doubted whether she was really taking in much of what was happening around her. She moved aside to let James into the room—fortunately it was a large bathroom by modern standards. James was fishing around in his bag to produce a syringe and an ampoule of a diuretic drug.

May hardly seemed to notice the injection. They waited for a few minutes, James constantly monitoring May's pulse, and Penny anxiously watching her breathing and colour. Gradually her lips became pink, and her breathing eased.

'All right, May, let's try and help you out of there,' said James, flicking a glance to Penny. Violet was still hovering anxiously behind them, offering encouragement to her sister every now and then. Penny stood up and murmured quietly, 'Has your sister got a warm dressing-gown she could put on instead of the blanket?'

Violet bustled out, pleased to have something to do. She returned in a moment with a bulky woollen gown, which Penny took from her with a smile of thanks.

'Now that you're not so breathless, May,' she said, 'do you think you can stand up?'

It took a good ten minutes of gentle encouragement to bring May to her feet, and, between the three of them, help her to step out of the bath safely. Penny had asked Violet to place a chair beside the bath so that May could rest and get her breath back, and at last—it seemed to take for ever—they had helped the old lady into bed. She lay, completely exhausted, propped up against a mound of pillows.

James sat on the edge of the bed, checking her pulse again. 'That was a nasty episode, May!' he said. 'I'd be a lot happier if you went into hospital for a few days.'

'Oh, no, Doctor!' May looked horrified. 'I don't want to go to hospital—let me die at home!'

James laughed. 'May, you're not going to die for a while. I want you to go to hospital so that we can give you the proper treatment for your heart, otherwise you're going to go on having bad turns like you did tonight. I don't think that's very fair on Violet, do you?'

The old lady thought for a few minutes, then, closing her eyes, shook her head. 'No, I don't want to cause my sister any trouble. How long do you think I'll have to stay in the hospital?' She opened her eyes slightly to look at him.

He smiled. 'Just a few days—a week, perhaps. I'll go and ring them now—I'd like you to go this evening.'

While James went downstairs to use the telephone, Penny helped Violet prepare a small overnight case for her sister. 'Do you think I'll be able to go with her?' Violet asked with a worried frown.

'Yes, of course—she'll be very glad of your company.'

'You've been so helpful.' Violet was close to tears. 'I didn't know what to do. . .'

'You did just the right thing,' Penny told her, trying to sound reassuring.

'Right,' said James, coming back up the stairs. 'An ambulance will be here in a few minutes, and the hospital is expecting you. I'll just write down the medicines I've given you. . .' He sat down to write his notes. 'I'll be back to see you as soon as you're home again—whoops! I'm in demand. . .' He reached into his pocket to silence the shrill tones of his bleeper. 'Violet, may I use your phone again?' He disappeared once more.

The packing complete, Penny sat on the bed and

checked May's pulse. It was slower and stronger than it
had been when she had sat so breathlessly in the bath,
and her general appearance was much improved.

'I've got to make another call,' said James, reappear-
ing. He looked doubtfully at Penny. 'It's on this side of
town—you'll have to come with me, or. . .'

'Perhaps I could wait here until the ambulance
arrives,' suggested Penny. 'You could collect me on your
way back.'

The ambulance arrived ten minutes after he had left.
As he had predicted, the Misses Soames seemed per-
turbed at the idea of two beefy ambulancemen climbing
their stairs, but when they saw that one of the crew was
a woman, they seemed happier. In a couple of minutes
May was installed in the back of the ambulance, with
Violet sitting opposite her clutching the holdall.

Penny said goodbye and saw them off. Back inside the
house she turned off the lights and made sure everything
was bolted and secure, just as she had promised Violet.
She waited by the front door until she heard James's car
draw up outside, then let herself out and locked the door
behind her.

'Thanks for waiting with them,' said James as they
drove back towards his house. 'They're nice old girls—
but I'm afraid they can't go on managing completely
alone like that. Something will have to be sorted out for
May's return—perhaps we can think about that on
Monday.'

'I hope May's going to be all right,' mused Penny.
'She seemed so frightened going off in the ambulance—
and Violet looked completely lost too. I almost wished I
was going with them.'

'What, and leave me to eat that lasagne all by myself?'
laughed James.

'I just hope it's fit to eat—we've been out over an hour!'

'I'm sure it'll be wonderful.' James was helping her out of the car.

Penny went straight to the kitchen to retrieve the now rather well-cooked pasta. 'It's a bit dry, but I think it's just about edible,' she called. 'I'll chuck some salad together, and we'll eat—OK?'

'Fine!' James appeared in the doorway and sniffed. 'Smells good—I'm hungry!' He produced plates and cutlery, and laid two places at the tiny table in the corner of the sitting-room.

Just as they sat down, the phone rang. They looked at one another in dismay. 'Oh, no!' groaned James. 'I wish I could ignore it, but I suppose I'd better answer. Just keep your fingers crossed that it's someone panicking over nothing.'

Penny hoped so—the last thing she wanted was for James to have to go out again. The evening was rapidly turning into a disaster. The way James was speaking into the phone warned her that this was not a time-waster but a genuinely serious call. Putting down the receiver, he turned to her with a worried frown.

'Sorry, Penny, I'll have to go out. Little Natalie Pearce—do you know her?—her mother's very worried. It sounds as if it might be meningitis. I'll be back as soon as I can.' He was by the open front door, but suddenly he turned and came back into the room to plant a firm but tender kiss on Penny's surprised lips.

'Don't go—please?' he murmured, his voice husky with longing and regret.

'I'll be here—I promise.' She gave him a little push. 'Now go and see Natalie.'

Alone, she looked pityingly at the lasagne, which was already past its best. 'It's back in the oven for you, I'm afraid,' she said aloud, carrying the dish back into the kitchen. 'You'll probably never get eaten, but we can live in hope!'

She washed up the pans which James had made her leave—more to pass the time than anything else. While she dabbled in the water she thought about Natalie Pearce—she was four years old, and had come into the surgery only a couple of weeks ago to have two stitches removed from a cut on her forehead. Penny remembered her clearly because she was such a chatterbox, and had not stopped talking from the time she entered the treatment-room to the time she left, even when Penny had been snipping the sutures.

The pans were washed and dried, the kitchen spotless, and Penny wandered aimlessly back into the sitting-room. It felt strange to be here alone, almost as if she was an intruder. She sat on the edge of a chair, wondering how long James was likely to be. Why had she promised to stay? She would rather go home—it was no fun sitting in a strange house, just waiting and waiting. . .

She got up and looked at his books. He had a huge collection of medical textbooks, and she thumbed through one or two, but they were very specialised, and she was in no mood to concentrate hard on understanding them. There were quite a few travel books, and some biographies of musicians, classical and jazz. Not much fiction, she mused with disappointment.

She tried to settle down with a book about India, but she found her attention constantly wandering to James, and wondering why he had been so long.

At last she heard his car grumble to a halt outside, and his key fumbled in the lock.

She was shocked by his appearance. His face was grey, his cheeks etched with deep lines. Barely an hour had passed since he had left the house, but he looked older and thinner.

'My goodness, James, what's happened?' she gasped, jumping up from her chair in concern.

Wearily he crossed the room and flopped into the other armchair. He sat, staring at the unlit fireplace, his eyes distant and lifeless.

'James. . .?'

Slowly he turned his eyes upon her. 'Natalie Pearce is a very sick child, Penny,' he said quietly. 'When I arrived she was displaying classic signs of meningitis—she was curled up, whimpering, couldn't bear the light, her neck was stiff. . . I waited with her parents for the ambulance. The damned thing took forever——' His voice rose angrily, and his fists clenched on the arms of the chair. Penny knelt down beside him.

'Will she be all right?'

He shook his head. 'I don't know. They'll do a lumbar puncture at the hospital—see whether the cause is viral or bacterial. I felt so helpless. The parents were looking at me—willing me to do something to help their child.'

Gently Penny laid her hands on his arm, feeling the tense knots of muscle beneath the sleeve of his shirt. 'You did the only thing you could do—you went straight out to see her, and got her into hospital. It's out of your hands now.'

James looked down at his hands, turning them over as if he had never seen them before. 'Healing hands. . .' he muttered bitterly, and, suddenly getting to his feet, smashed his fists against the mantelpiece.

Penny rose to her feet too, and without stopping to think offered instinctive comfort. Coming up behind him, she put her arms around his waist and leaned her cheek against his broad back. 'Ssh!' she whispered. 'Don't give up hope, James. You're a good doctor, but you can't help every single patient. . .not even when it's a child.'

For a moment he seemed to stand quite still, and she could feel his heart beating against her cheek. Then, in one whirling movement, he had turned around, and this time she was in his arms, and he was holding her so tightly that she had to fight for breath.

After a moment or two he seemed to realise that he was crushing her tiny frame, and his arms relaxed a little, but still he held her. 'Oh, Penny!' The words were barely audible. His mouth was close to her ear—she could feel his warm breath. 'Penny, thank goodness you're here! I need you—I need your strength. . .'

His lips claimed hers hungrily, passionately, and she felt as if he was drawing on her own reserves of power, leaving her weak and helpless. She returned his kisses with an involuntary eagerness. She was incapable of resisting—she didn't *want* to resist. This man excited her in a way she had never experienced before, not even with Chris.

James's caresses seemed to inflame every nerve in her body. Suddenly he straightened up and looked down at her upturned face. His eyes held a question that Penny instantly recognised. Her legs seemed about to melt, but desperately she fought to hang on to her common sense.

'I'm going home,' she said slowly, watching a variety of expressions cross James's face. 'You're tired and worried, and I think I should go and let you get some sleep.' She pulled away from his arms, reluctantly fending off his attempts to draw her close again. 'Sorry, James—my mind's made up.'

Releasing her at last, James passed a weary hand across his eyes. 'Look, Penny, it hasn't been quite the evening I'd hoped for. . .'

'Nonsense. It's been—well, *interesting*! And you won't *always* be on call. . .'

'No, thank goodness. Now come here and let me kiss you before you go. . .'

As she lay in a hot bath a little while later Penny thought about the little girl now fighting for her life in hospital. She prayed for a happy outcome, then allowed her mind to dwell on the surprising turn of events with a certain country GP.

Neil turned up at the surgery on Monday morning, looking pale and drawn, but insisting that he was well enough to work.

'Sorry about dumping the on-call on to you, James,' he said, as they all gathered in the kitchen for a pre-surgery cup of coffee. 'Hope it didn't muck up your weekend too much.'

'Well, I did have a date with someone rather special, but she's a very understanding young woman,' replied James, aiming a wink at Penny over Neil's shoulder.

'She'd have to be, to go out with a doc——' Neil's voice trailed off as he caught the look passing between James and Penny.

'Have I missed something?' he asked, bewildered.

'No, Neil. Come on, I'll go through the calls before we start work.' James breezed out of the kitchen, leaving Neil, still puzzled and frowning, to follow.

In a quiet moment Penny looked through her notes from Friday's seminar. Those lectures seemed to have been a long, long time ago. So much seemed to have changed since she and James had driven down to Bath just three days ago.

She was just about to leave that afternoon when Neil knocked on the treatment-room door and ambled inside.

He looked a bit better than he had that morning, she was pleased to see.

'I thought we might have a practice meeting tomorrow lunchtime,' he began. 'We can discuss any ideas you and James might have about setting up a diabetic clinic—I know he's keen. And I also want to review the over-seventy-fives—can you come up with a figure for this year's assessments?'

'Yes, of course. I think it's a good idea to have a meeting.' Penny expected Neil to go, but he hesitated in the doorway.

'Penny——'

She waited expectantly, her suspicions aroused as to what was coming next.

'Penny, tell me to mind my own business if you like, but is there something going on between you and James?'

She smiled and shrugged slightly. 'We've been seeing a bit of one another, yes,' she admitted, 'but it's not a big thing. We're just—friends. . .' She knew this didn't sound very convincing, and Neil continued to look doubtful.

'I hope your personal feelings aren't going to affect your working relationship, Penny.'

'I know you think it's a bad idea to become involved with a colleague, but I assure you this won't make any difference to the way we work together,' she assured him.

'I hope you're right,' said Neil, shaking his head gloomily.

The practice meeting was quite an eye-opener for Penny. The normal politeness between the members of the team went out of the window—this was the time for airing grievances, and there seemed to be plenty of them. The two doctors argued about how much time should be set aside for visiting patients in the local nursing homes. Joan complained that Neil hung on to his notes for too long when he wanted to refer patients to hospital consultants. Angela seemed to have a shopping list of grumbles, including one about Penny's habit of taking notes from the shelves and forgetting to put a marker in their place.

'Right,' said Neil, 'if everyone's finished having a moan, let's hear how Penny's getting on with the elderly assessments.'

Penny spoke for a few minutes about the assessments she had performed since she had joined the practice. 'I've looked at last year's figures,' she told the others, 'and we seem to be getting a slightly better take-up rate on this year's invitations, but it's a bit early to tell yet.'

'Good. We'll have another look at the numbers in three months' time. Now, James, what plans have you got for our diabetic care?'

'I'm keen to try organising a clinic—perhaps monthly to kick off with. Penny and I heard some very interesting ideas about transferring diabetic care from hospital to community at the seminar on Friday, and I think we were both inspired to rethink the way we handle diabetes in the practice—but the details will have to be sorted out. We haven't had time to come up with any definite plans yet.'

'Let's leave this, then, until you've worked out a way of incorporating an extra clinic into our surgery timetable—now, anything else?'

The meeting came to a close, and general chatter broke out. Neil was rushing off to make some calls, but James remained behind. Penny noticed how cheerful he seemed, and this was soon explained.

'I heard this morning—Natalie Pearce is on the mend!

She's responding very well to treatment, and shows no signs of permanent neurological damage!'

'That's fantastic!' Penny returned his wide smile. 'I'm so pleased for her parents—and for you! You look a lot happier than you did on Saturday night.'

'Speaking of Saturday, why don't you let me make up for that disaster by taking you out this evening?'

'I'd love to,' replied Penny without hesitation.

CHAPTER SEVEN

'WELL, come on, Penny, tell me all about it!' Jan lay on her sofa watching Penny expectantly.

'I've no idea what you mean,' said Penny, trying to look innocent.

'Rubbish! Neil told me that you and James can hardly keep your hands off each other. . .'

'Jan!' exploded Penny. 'He didn't say anything of the kind!'

'OK, so I'm exaggerating, but you know what I mean. So come on, girl—spill the beans! Goodness knows, I need a bit of gossip to cheer me up! Since I came out of hospital I feel as if I'm in a cocoon—completely cut off from the outside world.'

'Oh, dear—poor Jan!' Penny looked sympathetic, only to be rewarded with a sharp dig in the ribs from her friend.

'I'm waiting. . .'

Penny laughed. 'OK—James and I have been spending a bit of time together.'

'How much time?' demanded Jan.

'Oh——' Penny shrugged. 'Every evening when he's not on call.'

'Aha!' Jan looked serious. 'That sounds promising.'

'Oh, Jan, I didn't mean this to happen. I really wasn't ready to walk into another relationship after Chris.' Penny sighed. 'I'm still not sure if I'm doing the right thing.'

'The important thing is—how do you feel about

James?' Jan leaned forward, frowning a little as she pondered the problems of Penny's romance.

'I know he's quite an extraordinary person. He can be totally exasperating, but—so much fun!'

'In other words—you're in love with him.'

There was silence for a moment while Penny considered this bald statement. 'No. . .' she said thoughtfully, 'I don't think I'm in love with him—not yet. I'm still not free of the past, and until I am I can't let myself love anyone.'

'Have you told James about Chris?' asked Jan.

'No.'

'But he knows there was someone in London?'

'Yes. He's too sensitive to probe too much. That's one of the things I like about him,' Penny smiled.

Jan shook her head and threw up her hands in a gesture of despair. 'What did I tell you? It's love!'

Jan's words kept slipping back into Penny's mind over the next couple of days. Every time she saw James, she asked herself if it could be true—was she falling in love with him? Doggedly she denied it. It was too soon—it couldn't happen. She was determined that it *wouldn't* happen.

What she couldn't deny, though, was that she enjoyed James's company more and more. She breezed cheerfully through her work each day, looking forward to the evening, and the time she would spend with him.

'We'd better thrash out some details about this new clinic,' said James one afternoon, a few days after Penny's visit to Jan. 'This evening?'

Penny nodded. 'Sounds fine to me. How about another cookery lesson at the same time?'

This time their meal was not interrupted by the telephone, and Penny prepared chicken in a tangy sauce,

4 Free! Temptation romances

Plus a Free Teddy & Mystery Gift!

In heartbreak and in ecstasy Temptations capture all the bittersweet joys of contemporary romance.

And to introduce to you this powerful and fulfiling series, we'll send you *4 Temptation romances* absolutely **FREE** when you complete and return this card.

We're so confident that you'll enjoy Temptations that we'll also reserve a subscription for you, to our Reader Service, which means that you could enjoy...

- **4 BRAND NEW TEMPTATIONS** - sent direct to you each month (before they're available in the shops).

- **FREE POSTAGE AND PACKING** - we pay all the extras.

- **FREE MONTHLY NEWSLETTER** - packed with special offers, competitions, author news and much more...

Free Books and Gifts claim

Yes Please send me my 4 FREE Temptation romances together with my FREE gifts. Please also reserve a special Reader Service subscription for me. If I decide to subscribe, I will receive 4 superb new Temptations for just £7.00 every month, post and packing FREE. If I decide not to subscribe I shall write to you within 10 days. The FREE books and gifts will be mine to keep. I understand that I am under no obligation whatsoever. I may cancel or suspend my subscription at any time simply by writing to you. I am over 18 years of age.

1A3T

Name ————————————————

Address ————————————————

———————————— Postcode —————

Signature ————————————————

Offer expires 30th April 1993. One per household. The right is reserved to refuse an application and change the terms of this offer. Readers overseas and Eire, send for details. Southern Africa write to: Book Services International Ltd. P.O. Box 41654 Craighall Transvaal 2024. You may be mailed with offers from other reputable companies as a result of this application. If you would prefer not to share in this opportunity, please tick box ☐

MPS
MAILING
PREFERENCE
SERVICE

Mills & Boon Reader Service
FREEPOST
P.O. Box 236
Croydon
CR9 9EL

NO
STAMP
NEEDED

Send NO money now

with brown rice and a salad. James surprised her by expertly removing the bones from the raw chicken breasts.

'Where did you learn how to do that?' gasped Penny, her eyes wide as she watched him at work.

'My mother taught me. She was always trying to teach her boys how to cook, but this was the only bit I mastered, probably because at the time I had my heart set on being a surgeon! The secret is to use a really sharp knife——'

'Well, I'm most impressed—when I try to do that I just end up with lots of raggedy bits!'

'Oh, you poor thing!' mocked James, planting a kiss on the tip of her nose. 'Now, I've done my party piece. You'd better show me how to cook this stuff!'

While they ate they discussed their plans for the diabetic clinic.

'I can't see a way of fitting in an extra session without losing something that's already running,' said James. 'In fact, I don't think it's necessary in a practice the size of ours. My suggestion is to designate one health promotion clinic each month as a diabetic session, and see how that works. What do you think?'

Penny nodded. 'That sounds good. We're unlikely to have enough patients to warrant a separate clinic, and that way we can fill up any spare appointments with general health promotion if necessary.'

'I'm meeting the diabetic consultant at the hospital on Monday,' James told her. 'I know he's keen on shared care for his patients, so I don't anticipate any conflict there. He may want to know how experienced you are in this field, as you'll be carrying a lot of responsibility.'

'Well, you can tell him I've got two years' experience of diabetic in-patient care, and I've done the English

National Boards course. But, James——' She hesitated, frowning anxiously.

'What is it?'

'I'm not guaranteed to be around by the time this clinic gets off the ground. I don't know whether Jan's got relevant experience. . .'

James paused for a moment. 'I don't think that's a problem,' he said slowly. 'Jan's not coming back. She told me today, but her letter of resignation hasn't arrived yet, so no one knows officially.'

'Oh,' Penny pondered this news. 'So does that mean. . .?'

'You'll be offered a permanent contract. The job's yours, if you want it. Think about it.'

Penny knew she would have to do just that—think carefully—but a small glow of pleasure took hold just the same. She loved this job, and to know she had been doing it well enough to be offered the permanent position gave her a great sense of satisfaction.

Trying to quell her excitement and hide it from James, she asked casually, 'Are you surprised that Jan's resigned just now? I would have expected her to wait until after the baby's born.'

James shrugged. 'She definitely won't be able to go out to work for the rest of her pregnancy, but I gather she thinks it's time for a change anyway. Steven runs his own business, and she's going to work for him. She's taking on some of his paperwork while she's laid up.'

'Goodness, you know a lot! I saw Jan a couple of days ago, and she didn't mention any of this to me.'

'I dropped in for a cup of tea after my rounds today, and she told me all about it. She seemed pleased to have made a decision—I think it's been on the cards for a while. So,' James smiled, 'it looks as if it's you and I running the diabetic clinic!'

With the uncertainty of the future lifted, Penny felt able to make plans. 'Great! I'll get in touch with the diabetic specialist nurse from the General, and see if she can come in and advise us on setting up.'

'Good idea. Now, no more shop talk! Come and sit in a more comfortable chair.' James got up from the table where they had been sitting over their coffee, and led her to an armchair. Instead of taking the other seat himself, he sprawled on the floor at her feet.

Leaning on one elbow, he looked up at her. 'Tell me about your family. You never say much about them—in fact, you never say much about yourself at all!'

Penny hesitated, surprised. 'Don't I? Oh, well, there's precious little to tell! I'm an only child, I was brought up on the outskirts of London. My father's an engineer, and my mother's a teacher. When I was growing up my father always seemed to be away from home, travelling the world, setting up engineering projects. I didn't see much of him at all. My mother didn't think it was good for a child to keep moving about, so we stayed at home. Now they're both in Nigeria on a three-year contract.'

'You must miss them.'

'Yes—especially my mother. We're very close, having spent so much time on our own together. But the contract ends in a few months, and when my mother heard about Gran's illness she decided to come home before Dad.' Her eyes lit up with pleasure. 'She's just waiting for someone to take over her teaching job, so she could be on her way any time now. Meanwhile, I've got Gran to keep me on the straight and narrow!'

James grinned. 'Is that what she's doing? So how did you get into nursing?'

'Don't laugh—I had my tonsils out when I was nine, and I thought hospital was the most wonderful place! There were so many children to play with, and the nurses seemed terribly glamorous! I set my heart on becoming a nurse, based on that very unrealistic picture of hospital life! As soon as I left school I started my training at the Western—and I think you know the rest.'

James frowned. 'Not all of it—someone hurt you in London. . .'

Penny forced a light-hearted laugh. 'Don't let's talk about that! Anyway, I've told you my life story—now I want to hear yours.'

He shifted to a more comfortable position on the rug in front of the fireplace. 'It's all pretty conventional. I'll probably bore you to death—let's see. . .born in Berkshire. . .father died when I was three. . .mother remarried when I was twelve. . .stepbrother came to live with us. . .went to medical school. . .qualified. . . became a GP. . .met a beautiful practice nurse——

'Hey,' Penny laughed, 'slow down! You're leaving out great chunks—how many children in your family?'

'Just myself and Kit, my stepbrother. Like you, I was an only child, and I always longed for brothers and sisters. When Mother remarried my wish was granted— an instant four-year-old stepbrother!'

'But you were so much older—I would imagine that could be difficult. There could be resentments. . .'

'Yes—but surprisingly there weren't many. I really appreciated having a whole family around me, and I think I set myself up as some sort of "minder" for my little brother. I was eight years older, but instead of finding him a nuisance, I was fascinated by seeing him grow up. The only problem is that as he's got older, he's turned to me to bail him out of every bit of trouble he's found himself in—and he's got a nose for it, believe me!'

'It sounds as if he's always looked up to you,' observed Penny.

'Yes, I suppose so. Everything I've ever done, he's

wanted to do the same. He followed me into medicine, even got into the same medical school. I thought when he got married he might begin to take a bit more responsibility for himself, break away from relying on me, but——' James paused, his mouth set in an impatient line '—it seems I was wrong!'

Penny hardly dared to ask. 'Has he sorted out his—*problems*?'

James rolled his eyes. 'I'm beginning to think Kit is completely incapable of doing any such thing. The last I heard, he'd moved out—or, more likely, been kicked out—of his home, leaving his American wife and small baby to manage on their own. The ironic thing is that the nurse at the centre of all this has done a bunk.'

A tiny note of warning was sounding in Penny's head. 'What do you mean?' she asked.

'According to Susie, Kit's wife, this girl has disappeared from the scene, but instead of coming to his senses, Kit's trying to find her. The amount of trouble that little schemer has caused!'

'James——' Penny's voice was hoarse '—I've just realised. . .if Kit is your stepbrother, his surname isn't Yorke——'

'No—Freeman. Didn't I ever tell you that?'

'No—no, you didn't.' She was fighting to keep a note of panic at bay.

'What's the matter? You look surprised. Do you know him after all?'

Her thoughts were whirling. Kit—short for Christopher. Chris Freeman. Oh, hell.

James was looking at her expectantly. She forced an answer, surprising herself with the steadiness of her voice. 'I may know him. Have you got a photograph?'

There was a chance, wasn't there, a small chance that there were *two* Chris Freemans at the Royal Western

Hospital? Ignoring the total improbability, she clung to this forlorn hope while James rummaged around in the drawer of the little table and at last produced a handful of snapshots.

'Now let me see. . .' He shuffled through the snaps, and separated one from the rest. 'This was taken at his stag night, a couple of years ago. . .'

Penny hoped her face gave nothing away. Tentatively she took the proffered photograph and found herself looking at two laughing faces—James, more dishevelled than she had ever seen him, with his arm around the shoulders of a younger man, his stepbrother, and Penny's ex-lover.

'Well?' James was smiling.

'I—um—I think I know him. Yes, I've seen him around the hospital.' Penny could barely raise her voice above a whisper.

James took back the picture, and looked closely into her face, frowning a little. 'Penny, are you all right? You don't look too well. . .'

'Yes—well, no, actually. I'm not feeling too wonderful. I think perhaps I'd better go home.'

'I'll drive you.' He looked really concerned now.

'No, really, James, it's not necessary. I'll be fine in the car. I just feel a bit off colour.'

He saw her out to her Mini, still frowning. 'I hope you're going to be all right—I wish you'd let me drive. Anyway,' he added, leaning his head in at the window while she fastened her belt, 'think about the job over the weekend. I won't see you until Monday. I'm going to London to see if I can find my fool of a brother and talk some sense into him.'

Penny stared at him, aghast. 'You're going to visit him—this weekend?'

'Yes. Sorry I didn't tell you earlier. I'll mention your name, if you like—see if he remembers you. . .'

'No!' she almost shouted, regaining control at the last moment. 'I mean—I think you'd be wasting your breath.'

James leaned forward and kissed her cheek. 'You don't seem yourself at all—go home to bed. I hope you're not going down with the virus that's been going around.'

With a brief wave she pulled away. All the way to Fernhill she made a supreme effort to concentrate on the road, but once inside her room in the cottage she let her thoughts go free.

How could it happen? Of all the people in the world, all the doctors—she had to end up working for the brother of the man who had made her life a misery. Working for him, and caring for him too, she realised.

One thing was clear—she was going to have to tell James the truth. But when? It was probably already too late. Tomorrow morning he would be on his way to London, and when he had given his brother a lecture on fidelity, he'd say, 'By the way, our new practice nurse came from the Western—Penny Lambert—do you know her?'

It wasn't going to be necessary to tell James, because by the time she saw him on Monday he was going to know—to know that she was the 'little schemer', the 'marriage-wrecker' who had seduced his precious stepbrother and dragged him down the rocky road to separation and perhaps divorce. . .

She spent a miserable weekend going over and over everything in her mind. This was the end of her job at the surgery—the job which hadn't even been officially offered to her yet. She doubted whether any such offer would be made now, and even if it was, it would obviously be impossible to stay.

Oh, why did I ever have to set eyes on Chris Freeman? Penny asked herself time and time again. In fact, why did I have to set eyes on James? They're both more trouble than they're worth.

She greeted Monday with great trepidation. Once at the surgery, she went straight to the treatment room, hoping to put off for as long as possible the inevitable moment when she would have to see James.

He sent her one or two patients during the morning. His voice on the telephone was cool and businesslike, as it always was during working hours. It was an exceptionally busy morning. After a succession of blood tests Penny removed some stitches from the neck of a patient who had had a suspicious little lump removed, and re-dressed a nasty dog bite which had become infected. A young woman came to ask for advice about giving up smoking, and Penny spent some time talking to her and gave her some leaflets to read.

By the end of the morning she felt punch-drunk with the number and variety of patients she had seen. She found the necessity of being able to provide advice on so many different problems quite a strain.

Neil appeared, and she tried to explain how she was feeling.

'I'm not an expert on everything under the sun,' she moaned, feeling sorry for herself.

'You don't need to be—no one expects it of you,' said Neil soothingly.

'The patients do! They think I'm going to be able to answer any question they throw at me. . .'

'The important thing is that you know how to *obtain* the information you need—or where to send the patient to get their questions answered.' Neil looked at her

kindly. 'You're doing fine, Penny—in fact, the job is
yours permanently if you want it! Jan has written to say
that she doesn't want to return, so I'd be very pleased if
you'd consider staying with us.'

'Is James in favour of offering the job to me?' she
asked, surprised that he had not already vetoed the idea.

'Of course—we're both pleased with the way you've
fitted into the team. James has worked alongside you
more than I have, and he's very confident that you're the
right person for the job.'

Penny bowed her head in thought. So James hadn't
said anything to Neil yet. She hadn't seen him this
morning—she had no way of knowing whether her secret
was still intact or not. 'Is James here?' she asked Neil.

'No—he went off after surgery to see the diabetic
specialist at the General.'

'Oh yes, of course! He told me about his meeting. . .
Listen, Neil—can I have time to think this over? I'm
very grateful to you for offering me the contract. I love
the work here. It's just—I have to do some thinking,
revise my plans. . .'

'Naturally. I quite understand. Let's say—an answer
by the beginning of next week?'

Penny nodded, and Neil departed on his rounds.

She had been telling the truth—she did have some
serious thinking to do. How could she accept the job
without knowing whether James had found her out?

He would be back from his meeting by two o'clock,
she knew, because that was when she carried out the
children's immunisations, and James was always there to
check that each child was fit to receive the injection.

There were eight on the list for this afternoon's clinic,
but experience had shown Penny that usually two or
three did not turn up, because the children had colds or
the mother had forgotten the appointment. Penny always

made a point of telling the mothers that the children could still have their injections if they had a cold unless they were running a high temperature, or had an upset stomach. Even so, each week a message came through to say that so-and-so would not be coming because they had the snuffles.

By the time the children arrived at Penny's door they had already seen the doctor, but she always ran her own checks before administering the vaccination.

'Is Gemma well at the moment?' she asked a harassed-looking mother with a two-month-old baby in her arms and a toddler rampaging around the room. Gently Penny pointed the sturdy little boy in the direction of the toys she always brought out for this clinic.

She enquired about recent contact with infectious diseases, serious allergies, or a family history of epilepsy. While she prepared the injection she gave advice about the slight reaction which could be expected, and how to deal with it.

'Can you hold Gemma firmly on your knee, like this. . .' She showed Gemma's mother how to tuck in her arms and legs so that she couldn't jerk when the needle went in.

Deftly she gave the injection. After a moment's pause the expected wail came, and Gemma's mother laughed and comforted her baby daughter, relieved that it was over.

Penny didn't like doing the immunisations, especially, like this, the first of the 'triples', the course of three injections which protected against diphtheria, tetanus and whooping cough. Poilio vaccine was delivered by mouth, and she gave this now to Gemma, who was still crying. 'Here you are, sweetheart — a couple of drops on your tongue. . .'

Gemma screwed up her face and cried again, but the

liquid seemed to have gone down, and Penny signed the medical card and the record book which Gemma's mother had been given at the baby clinic.

'See you again in a month, then, Gemma!' Penny gave the baby's hand a little squeeze, and opened the door for the family to go out and the next to come in.

Two months old seemed so tiny to be starting on injections, but Penny was well aware of the importance of all children being immunised against these potentially serious diseases. She had seen babies with whooping cough during her student days. There had been one of the periodic epidemics while she was on the children's ward, and it was pitiful to see the babies fighting for their breath. The serious side-effects of such illnesses in very young children or in those unable to fight infections, such as children being treated for leukaemia, had been drummed into her during her training, and again by James when she had first joined the practice. So each week she cheerfully gave the injections, dished out stickers and the occasional sweet, and hid her natural abhorrence of sticking needles into children. They almost always cried, and she hated feeling that she was the cause of their distress.

The next baby was three months old, and was returning for his second injection. He was followed by a four-year-old for a pre-school booster, and twins of a little over a year who needed MMR—measles, mumps and rubella. Their mother was anxious because she had forgotten to mention something to James.

'They were making such a racket in there that it completely went out of my mind,' she told Penny. 'Oliver has had German measles, about three months ago, but Thomas didn't get it. Does it make any difference?'

Penny shook her head. 'None at all, Mrs Long. It

won't do Oliver any harm to be given the vaccine, even though he may already be immune to rubella—German measles.'

Immunising twins was not easy, but somehow they managed, and at last the waiting area was clear and Penny returned the vaccines to the fridge where they were stored. Then she turned her attention to the inevitable paperwork. She had signed the medical notes as she had gone along, but there were other records to be completed, and she knew that if she didn't do it straight away, something vital would be overlooked. It was so easy to forget to write things down.

She was absorbed in this task when the door opened behind her and James stepped quietly into the room. In fact, she wasn't aware of his presence until two arms wrapped themselves around her and a soft kiss was planted on her neck, just behind her ear. A delicious shiver ran down the length of her back.

'Well, have you accepted the job?' murmured James, still nuzzling her ear. 'Please tell me you're going to stay—I couldn't bear to hear that you're going to disappear out of my life.'

Penny couldn't believe her ears. So effectively had she convinced herself that James would soon be ranting at her, declaring her an evil marriage-wrecker and just about any other name he could think of, that this warm and amorous approach had caught her quite off balance.

'I—er—I've got until this time next week to think about it.'

'What is there to think about? You enjoy the job, don't you?'

'Yes, very much, but things aren't that simple, James.'

He released her, and suddenly swung round to sit on the chair beside her desk. 'Tell me about it,' he invited.

She shook her head. 'No. I've got to sort out what's

best in my own mind. It's my life, my career, and I'm going to make the decisions on my own.'

James pulled a face. 'You're very independent, Miss Lambert. Very determined to keep all your troubles to yourself. What does it take to get you to talk, to open up?'

'Who said anything about troubles?' Penny frowned. 'The point is, I only came here to stay with Gran when she was ill. I've got to decide whether this is what I really want.'

'You seemed enthusiastic enough the other evening when we were planning the diabetic clinic. What's happened to change your mind?'

'Nothing!' snapped Penny. James's perception made her nervous. 'I just want time to think, without people putting pressure on me all the time!'

He looked at her coldly. 'Presumably by "people" you mean me. I suppose our relationship has no bearing on the issue? I've told you how I feel about you—isn't that of any importance?'

'Of course! But——' She spluttered to a halt.

James took over. 'But you've got to consider whether there's any room in your "career plan" for a relationship with a country GP. OK, Penny, I'll leave you to make your mind up. Perhaps you'd be good enough to let me know your decision—preferably before I hear it from Neil!'

He slammed out of the room. Damn! thought Penny, sitting hunched over her desk, her head in her hands.

In his own room across the corridor, James slumped into his chair, adopted the same attitude of despair, and uttered a single word aloud. 'Damn!'

A few minutes after James had gone Penny suddenly realised that she still had no idea what had happened in

London at the weekend. Had he seen Chris? Had he mentioned her name?

Presumably not, as he had made no mention of it. Had he found out that she was the 'other woman' he would certainly have created hell, and probably chucked her straight out of the surgery. No—either he hadn't seen Chris, or her name had not come up in their conversation.

But how long was she going to be able to keep the whole affair a secret from him? Surely, surely it was only a matter of time. He was bound to find her out, probably sooner rather than later. She didn't see how she could possibly stay here. But she *wanted* to so much! This was an opportunity which would have seemed heaven-sent in any other circumstances. Now it had a tinge of irony which seemed far from celestial in origin.

She would have to turn down the job—that took care of that decision. But far harder was the choice she had to make about James. To tell him the truth, or not? And if not, how was she to end their friendship—what excuses to make, what lies to tell?

The first thing to do, she decided, was to open up a gap between them, initiate a cooling-off process which would make it easier to tell him in due course that she had changed her mind; she didn't return his feelings——

But she would have to be quick, if she was going to make the break and go before she was thrown out in disgrace.

CHAPTER EIGHT

JAMES breezed into the treatment-room the following lunchtime in a cheerful mood. He had evidently decided to forget Monday's tiff and resume their previous affability. Penny started to return his friendly smile, but stopped herself. Instead she gave him a cool look. 'Hello, James. I'm almost ready.' The well woman clinic was about to begin. 'The notes are there, if you want to have a look—I'm just getting some request forms ready.' She bent her head again to the forms she was filling in.

'Good.' James's tone was easy—he didn't appear to have noticed her change of mood. 'Let's have a look. . . you should be able to manage all these on your own— oh. . .' he was flicking through the notes '. . .perhaps I'd better see Mrs Daker—she's been referred for colposcopy. She wants to know more about it. Will you call me in when she's here?'

Penny murmured her agreement, not meeting his eye. If James was aware by now of a difference in her attitude towards him, he did not comment.

The clinic began. It wasn't heavily booked, so Penny was able to spend plenty of time giving advice about diet and smoking. Two of the women were not due for a smear test, but wanted to be shown how to examine themselves for breast lumps. One turned out to need a tetanus booster, so Penny gave that at the same time.

She was becoming quite adept at taking the cervical smears, and the two booked in this afternoon caused her no problems. She found it a good time to chat about general health worries, and sometimes picked up other small problems during the course of this clinic.

Mrs Daker was last on the list. She had had a routine smear test about seven months earlier, which had turned out to be slightly abnormal. The lab had requested a repeat test after six months, and this had been one of Penny's first tasks when she had arrived at the practice. The result had again shown some abnormality, and this time the lab had recommended that Mrs Daker should be referred to the hospital for colposcopy.

Mrs Daker looked worried. 'I don't like the sound of it, Sister,' she said. 'Does it mean I've got cancer? I'm scared—my kids are so young. . .'

'The cervical smear test isn't just to test for cancer, Mrs Daker,' explained Penny. 'It's to pick up the smallest changes in the cells around the cervix—changes which start a long time before cancer develops. If we can detect these earliest changes, we can send you for simple treatment before there's any sign of cancer. That's why all women are encouraged to have regular tests.'

She knew she had told Mrs Daker all this last time, but in her distress and anxiety she seemed to have forgotten.

'But what is a colposcopy? It sounds horrible!'

James had crept quietly into the room while Penny was talking, and now he took over, explaining how the gynaecologist at the hospital would be able to have a look at the cervix through a microscope and identify the problem area.

'You may be able to have treatment almost immediately, as an outpatient,' he added, 'or sometimes it means an overnight stay. I can't say, I'm afraid. But try not to worry too much—you were sensible and came regularly for tests. Cervical cancer is quite preventable if these early changes are spotted.'

Penny found some information leaflets for Mrs Daker to read at home, and was pleased to see that she looked a little happier as she left the surgery.

'It must be hard not to worry,' said Penny thought-fully, imagining herself in the same situation. 'I hope she doesn't have to wait too long for an appointment at the hospital!'

'I'm afraid they're a bit slow at the moment.' James pulled a face. 'She probably won't be seen for at least two months.'

Penny was horrified. 'That's far too long!' she cried furiously. 'How can they expect these women to put up with that kind of delay. . .?'

'Hey, calm down!' laughed James, holding out his hands defensively. 'That's nothing compared to the waiting list this time last year. They've taken on another gynae consultant since then. I agree with you that it's bad, but all we can do is offer support to our patients while they're waiting.'

Penny shrugged her agreement. 'I suppose so. I'm surprised they're not all in here demanding tranquillisers!'

'Well, they wouldn't get them from me, anyway,' smiled James. 'I don't hold with using drugs to solve people's anxieties—if you take the time to talk, you can usually find a more practical way of helping.'

As she watched him, his face serious as he considered his patients and their worries, Penny's heart jumped. How was she going to pretend that she didn't care for this man? The longer she spent with him, the more times they worked together, the stronger her feelings for him became.

He stood up to leave. She had to ask—she couldn't bear not knowing. . .

'How did you get on at the weekend. . .with your stepbrother?'

'Not too well. He was on call at the hospital, and I only managed to see him for a few minutes—hardly long enough to sort anything out. I spent longer with his wife. She's in a terrible state, poor girl. Her parents in Boston have already sent her an air ticket home, and I think she's going to go. Their baby daughter's only three months old, for goodness sake! I'd wash my hands of Kit if it wasn't for his family. Someone's got to try and sort the idiot out, for their sake!'

Penny tried to block out all that he was saying about Chris's wife and baby—knowing about them was just too painful. Instead she concentrated on the fact that they had only had a few minutes together. Not long enough to get on to general chat, surely? She couldn't ask James, 'Did you mention me?' She would have to assume that he hadn't—and also assume that Chris hadn't volunteered the name of the infamous nurse. If he had, James wouldn't be looking at her now with such a fond expression.

'Penny, let's go out somewhere this evening!'

'No, James.' She watched bewilderment cross his face, and continued, 'I—I don't think we should see so much of one another. Outside work, I mean.'

He was frowning. 'What's happened to change your mind, Penny? A few days ago you were happy to spend your time with me—have I upset you somehow?'

'No, James, it's nothing like that.'

'Is it Neil—has he said something to you? I know he's got hopelessly old-fashioned ideas about keeping business and pleasure totally separate. You mustn't take too much notice——'

'No, James!' said Penny firmly. 'Please believe me, I just think it's best. I don't think there's any future for us.' She dragged the words out, each one seeming to inflict its own pain as she spoke.

James looked shocked. He took a step towards her and put both hands on her shoulders, his inquisitive blue eyes searching deep into hers. 'What is it, Penny? What are you afraid of?'

She forced herself to meet his gaze, even though she really wanted to shut her eyes and keep her emotions safely hidden away. 'I'm not afraid—just realistic,' she whispered. 'I can't. . .return your feelings.'

He continued to watch her. She wanted to shake off those strong, warm hands and back away, but she stood her ground.

Suddenly James's lips were on hers, taking her completely by surprise. His kiss, initially hard and demanding, quickly became soft and sweet, teasing and tempting her to yield to him.

Doggedly suppressing his instinctive reactions, she remained unresponsive, eventually reaching up and pushing him away. They stood a couple of feet apart, breathing heavily and glaring at one another.

James spoke at last. 'I see. Or rather I don't see, but you've made your point.' At that he left the room, and she was able to sink on to her chair, her legs weak and shaking.

Afternoon surgery was about to begin. Penny longed for the day to be over, but she still had an hour and a half until she could go home. A child with a cut chin needed two stitches removed; a postman had a nasty gash on his hand from a rusty nail on someone's garden gate. Penny cleaned the wound, used a 'butterfly' tape to hold the edges together, and checked on the date of his last tetanus booster. A further dose wasn't necessary, which pleased the postman.

Rashes, bandages, blocked ears—for the first time

since she had taken on this job Penny felt a twinge of impatience with all these people. She wanted to finish and get out of the surgery—put some distance between herself and James.

At last it was time to go. Usually the last thing she did was to tidy the room carefully and check for any low stocks of supplies so that the ordering could be done in the morning. Today she swept all the odd scraps of paper from the desk into the top drawer and left the room without a backward glance.

James still had patients to see, but Neil had finished and was in reception gathering up notes for his urgent calls.

'Penny, just a minute. I'll walk with you to your car.' He caught her up and fell into step beside her. 'You don't look happy today,' he commented. 'Any problems at work?'

'No,' she answered briefly. The last thing she wanted at the moment was for Neil to start probing.

'Good. So you're still considering the job?'

They had reached Penny's Mini. 'I haven't made up my mind yet, Neil—you said I could have until Monday——'

'Of course, of course—but I'm not blind, Penny. You look tense, and James looks furious—I don't know what the problem is, and I don't want to know. I just want a team who can concentrate on their patients instead of their love-lives!'

With that reprimand he crossed to his own car, unlocked it and climbed in, leaving Penny to stare after him with tears of self-pity stinging her eyes.

She sat behind the driving wheel, sniffing a little. As she brushed the tears away, she thought seriously about Neil's words. This was what he had tried to warn her about—personal relationships getting in the way of work.

She sat for a few minutes, deep in thought. At last, she realised that if she didn't make a move she was in danger of running into James, whose car was parked just in front of hers. His surgery would be over any minute now.

Supper that evening was a quiet affair. Penny was inclined to be preoccupied with her own thoughts, but her grandmother too was strangely subdued. Clearing away the plates, Penny realised that Margaret had hardly eaten a thing.

'I'm just not hungry, darling,' she told Penny. 'I've got a bit of a summer cold, I think.'

Penny, alarmed, looked more closely at her grandmother. She reached out and laid a hand on Margaret's arm—the skin was dry and warm, but not feverish.

'There's nothing to worry about, Penny.' Margaret brushed away her hand and walked towards the stairs. 'But I think I'll have an early night—try to sleep this thing off.'

'Good idea. I'll bring you a drink and some aspirins.'

When Penny took a hot drink upstairs, the old lady was asleep. Tiptoeing out of the bedroom, she quelled a small ripple of alarm. It was probably, as Gran had said, just a light cold. If Margaret was sensible, and took care of herself, there was no reason why it should develop into anything more worrying.

The following morning Penny looked in on her grandmother before leaving for work. It was unusual for Margaret Lambert to stay in bed—she was usually up and dressed by half-past six—but she was awake and quite cheerful, accepting with delight the tray of tea and toast Penny had prepared.

'What luxury!' she cried, taking the tray on to her

knees. 'I'm a lazy old woman this morning, but I don't want to be carted off in an ambulance again, so I thought I'd better pamper this silly cold!'

'Quite right!' Penny nodded. 'I think I'd better stay at home today——'

Mrs Lambert wouldn't hear of her taking the day off. They finally reached a compromise—she would stay in bed until lunchtime, when Penny would pop home to see how she was feeling.

'I don't know how your patients stand your bossiness!' grumbled Margaret.

Penny laughed. 'They don't have to—none of them are as stubborn as you!'

When she arrived at work Penny found a message on her desk telling her that the diabetic specialist nurse would be calling in at the surgery at twelve-thirty to meet her and James, and offer advice on setting up their clinic. Penny's heart sank—she wouldn't have time now to go home between the morning and afternoon surgeries.

Debbie, the Specialist Nurse, arrived promptly. She was enthusiastic about the clinic idea, and was particularly pleased to hear that Penny was already well qualified in the subject.

'That's excellent,' she said. 'You'll know exactly what you're looking for. Have you drawn up a protocol?'

James produced a copy of the protocol he and Penny had prepared, and Debbie quickly read through it, nodding her approval. 'Looks fine. It's useful to me to see exactly what you propose to do, because with shared care I'm going to be seeing your patients at the hospital from time to time. We don't want to double up on some investigations and leave others out completely. Is this the record card you'll be using?'

They chatted on for a while. At last Debbie stood up

to leave. Penny took a surreptitious look at her watch—too late to go home and see Gran now.

'I'd like to drop in on a session when your clinic is established,' said Debbie, shaking hands with James. 'If you don't think I'd be too much of a nuisance?'

'Not at all,' he told her. 'That would be a great help. You can put us right if we're not coming up to scratch!'

He was enjoying himself, Penny realised, putting his ideas into action—seeing his plans take shape. She wished she could feel more enthusiastic about the project, but her future seemed so uncertain.

'Well?' As the door closed behind Debbie, James turned to Penny with a wry smile. He leaned against the dressings cupboard and folded his arms. 'Well?' he repeated. 'Does this mean you're staying? It seems I'm pretty much committed to running this diabetic session now——'

'But not necessarily with me. You could always advertise for a nurse with the relevant experience,' snapped Penny, irritated by the constant pressure James was putting on her to make a decision.

He bowed his head, and she frowned, wondering what was going through his mind. She looked at him standing there, strong arms folded casually. He had taken off his jacket, and in his crisp, finely striped shirt he looked vigorous and powerful. His deep red silk tie was a little askew, spoiling what would otherwise have been an immaculate image, and giving him a slightly raffish appearance.

Suddenly he looked up, catching her off guard as she gazed at him. Embarrassed, she turned away, not wanting him to see how much he attracted her.

'I really don't understand you, Penny.' His voice was low and quiet, husky with disappointment. 'You were so keen on this idea—we planned it all out together.

Without your enthusiasm, I probably wouldn't have pushed to get this clinic off the ground. Goodness knows, I've got enough to worry about at the moment. . .but knowing that you had the experience, and the will to make this work—that made all the difference. I thought we were going to make a good team, Penny—but now you're telling me that I may need to advertise for another nurse. Well, I don't think that's really on, do you? After all, the clinic isn't running yet. If you decide not to take the job, then I'll shelve the clinic for the time being.'

Penny was incredulous. 'Are you saying that the future of the diabetic clinic depends upon me staying? That's a form of blackmail!'

'Of course it isn't! Don't be so dramatic! It's practical common sense. If we have to find a new practice nurse, the chances are we'll find it hard to get anyone with general practice experience, never mind insisting on a certificate in diabetic nursing as well. I think we'd better stick to basics, and add the frills when we're in a position to do so.'

'But that's crazy—you've got approval for the clinic, we've done all the preparatory work—why chuck in the idea? As far as I can see, if you've got to find a new nurse, you may as well get someone with the background you need right at the beginning. Otherwise you may be stuck for years and years. . .'

James looked at her for a moment before replying. 'We've got someone with the right background already. It's hanging on to her which is proving difficult. . .'

Penny didn't want to pursue this any further. They were just going round and round in circles. She looked at her watch. 'We'll have patients arriving in a moment. I promise, James, you'll have my decision in a few days . . .don't try pressuring me into staying—I warn you, it'll probably have the opposite effect!'

She stood in the middle of the room, glaring at him. He looked at the tiny figure, her mannish check shirt tucked into a plain cotton skirt. The colour had risen on her cheeks as she had delivered the last words, and her hazel eyes had darkened with emotion. What was it, he asked himself silently, that she was always running away from?

With a sigh, he straightened up and put his hands on his hips. His expression was tense, watchful. 'I give up, Penny.' He shook his head sadly. 'I thought we had something pretty special starting between us, but I seem to have been mistaken. You won't even talk to me. Something's obviously bothering you, but you don't trust me enough to share it with me. . .'

Penny couldn't meet his eyes. His words hit home so accurately, and the pain in his voice seemed to wrench at her heart. But still she couldn't contemplate revealing the real reason for her coldness.

After a moment's awkward silence, James swept from the room, slamming the door behind him. Penny groaned inwardly—she was making things worse and worse! Soon they would not even be on speaking terms, and for what reason? Why was she throwing away this chance of happiness—all because of his selfish, cheating brother!

At the end of surgery she hastily cleared up and headed home as quickly as she could, anxious about her grandmother. She had tried to ring during the afternoon, but there had been no reply. That might mean, of course, that Gran was much better and had gone out, but she doubted whether that was very likely. Perhaps she had been asleep, or just not bothering to get out of bed to answer the call. Whatever the reason, Penny hoped it was an innocent one. Still she couldn't help worrying, and the ten-minute drive from Ellminster to Fernhill seemed endless.

She let herself into the house with a sinking feeling. 'Gran!' she called up the stairs, dropping her sweater and bag in the hall and starting to gallop up the steps two at a time. 'Gran, are you all right?'

She opened the bedroom door quietly, in case the old lady was asleep. One glance at the restless figure in the bed confirmed her fears. There was definitely something wrong.

Mrs Lambert lay on her side, her eyes closed and a high spot of colour on her cheek. She hadn't touched the jug of fruit juice Penny had left for her that morning. It looked as if she had been sleeping most of the day.

Penny sat on the side of the bed and gently took hold of one thin wrist. The skin was hot and the pulse weak and rapid. As far as she could judge, her grandmother had developed another chest infection. It was too soon after the recent bout of pneumonia—she wasn't yet fully strong.

'Gran!' She tried to rouse the old lady, shaking her shoulder firmly and speaking close to her ear. After a moment or two the eyes flickered open, and Mrs Lambert seemed to look at her granddaughter.

'Judith. . .?' The voice was quavering—quite unlike Margaret's usual firm tone. For a moment Penny couldn't think who Judith was, and then she remembered—Margaret's daughter, Penny's aunt, who had died some ten years ago.

'No, Gran,' she said clearly. 'It's Penny—I'm here to look after you.'

'Judith,' muttered her grandmother, her eyes closing again. 'You said you'd come on Saturday. . . I don't like that skirt. . .'

She was rambling, delirious, Penny realised. She

cursed the fact that she hadn't been able to get back here at lunchtime—perhaps if she'd seen then that Gran was developing a fever, things wouldn't have got this bad.

After a fruitless attempt to get Margaret to sip a drink, she went straight to the phone and dialled carefully. James was on call this evening, but would he be at home yet? He might have been making some house calls after surgery. She drummed her fingers while she waited, listening to the ringing tone.

'Hello?'

She was surprised to hear his voice, expecting the answering service to cut in. 'Oh—er—James!' she stuttered, feeling foolish. 'It's Gran—she's got another chest infection—at least, I'm pretty sure. . .she's in bed, delirious. I can't get any fluid into her, or anything. . .'

Aware that she sounded totally unprofessional, she was comforted by James's matter-of-fact tone. 'Right, I'll be over as soon as possible. Can you try and get her temp down a bit? Use a fan or something. See you in a minute——'

Penny knew there wasn't an electric fan in the house, but there were other things she could do to try and reduce Margaret's high temperature. Back in the bedroom, she stripped off the blankets and left her grandmother with just a sheet on top. She opened the window, welcoming the slight breeze which blew into the room. She didn't like the way Margaret was breathing, and tried to prop her up with another couple of pillows, but the old lady was so restless that she just kept sliding down again, and Penny had to content herself with making her as comfortable as possible.

A firm rap on the front door sent her flying down the stairs. She flung it open and practically dragged James inside.

'Oh, James—thank goodness! I don't like the look of

her at all!' She followed him up the stairs, still gabbling breathlessly. 'It's my fault—I said I'd come home at lunchtime, but we had that meeting. . .if I'd been here she wouldn't have got this bad. . . I didn't want to leave her this morning, but she——'

'Penny!' James turned to her and seized her by the shoulders, frowning into her face. With a little shake, he brought her to her senses. 'Stop talking and give me a hand!'

'Oh—yes—sorry. . .' she murmured meekly, crossing to the other side of the bed and helping to position her grandmother so that he could listen to her chest.

At last he straightened up, a worried line creasing his forehead. 'You're right—there seems to be some consolidation in both lungs. That last episode of pneumonia has left her very vulnerable to chest infections. She needs to be in hospital, Penny. You stay with her while I phone for an ambulance.'

Penny sat, holding her grandmother's hand, while she waited for the ambulance to arrive. She didn't know what James had told them, but they were there within minutes. He had waited with her, constantly checking his patient's condition. They said little.

As she took her seat in the back of the ambulance, she turned a wan face towards James, who was standing in the road. 'Thank you, James,' she said, her voice hardly more than a whisper.

He smiled reassuringly. 'There's nothing to thank me for—she's a tough old thing, she'll pull through.'

'I hope you're right.' Penny bit her lip, and turned to look at the blanket-swathed figure on the stretcher opposite her. The doors were closed, and they were on their way to Ellminster General.

Margaret was seen by the medical registrar and re-admitted to the ward which had looked after her previously. Some of the nurses on duty remembered their old patient, and Penny was pleased with the attention she received. It was always an eye-opener to see hospitals from the patients' and relatives' point of view, but there was nothing she could fault in the care given to her grandmother that evening.

Later, sitting at the bedside with a welcome cup of tea, she realised that she was exhausted. It had been a long and tiring day, and, glancing at her watch, she realised with surprise that it was ten o'clock. She hadn't eaten since breakfast, yet it was not hunger but an overwhelming weariness which seemed to descend on her like a heavy weight.

Margaret was wearing an oxygen mask to help her troubled respirations, and an intravenous infusion stopped her becoming dehydrated while she was so feverish and unable to drink. She had already been given a large dose of antibiotics, and the portable X-ray machine had been brought up to the ward to take an urgent chest X-ray. The staff nurse looking after Margaret had placed a fan beside the bed, and already the high temperature was coming down. Penny, satisfied that her grandmother's condition seemed more stable, closed her eyes for a moment. . .

'Penny——' The voice was unsteady and muffled by the plastic mask, but that one word was the most welcome sound Penny could have heard. She jumped up from her chair and leaned over the bed, smiling in delight.

'I'm here, Gran.'

Margaret's eyes were half open, and she seemed to be struggling to focus on Penny's face, but compared to her delirious state earlier that evening, she looked much better.

'Don't try and talk,' murmured Penny, smoothing a

lock of grey hair away from Margaret's eyes. 'Just rest, and get well. You're going to be fine!'

The pale blue eyes closed wearily, and Margaret slept. Penny sat for another half-hour, but clearly her grand-mother was sleeping deeply now, and unlikely to come to for the next few hours.

She had a word with the staff nurse, making sure that she would be called immediately if there was any cause for concern.

Downstairs in the main entrance the night porter called her a taxi, and by the time she reached the cottage she felt as if she could barely drag her feet up the path to the front door.

She sank into a chair in the sitting-room, too tired to take herself upstairs to bed. For a while she just sat there, staring blankly into space, wondering what would have happened if she hadn't been around—if Margaret had still been living alone. . .

She was vaguely aware of the sound of a car pulling up in the lane, but the double rap on the front door made her jump. She looked at her watch—almost eleven-thirty! Who on earth would be calling at this time of night?

Quietly she crossed to the window and peered out from behind the closed curtains. If she craned her neck she could just see the porch, illuminated by the outside light. . .

James. She gave a sigh of relief, noticing for the first time that her heart was thumping wildly. Quickly she ran out to the hall to let him in.

'Goodness, you gave me a fright! I couldn't imagine who would be calling at this hour—I thought I was about to be attacked by some weirdo——'

James shook his head apologetically. 'Sorry to scare you—I was on a call in the village, and I saw your light was on, so I stopped. I tried ringing you an hour or so ago, so I knew you must have only just got back. How's Margaret?'

Penny filled him in on her grandmother's condition, smiling when she told him how the old lady had woken up and recognised her.

'That's a good sign. She must be responding to the treatment already. It's likely to take some time for her to fully recover, though.'

This sounded like a warning, and Penny bristled. 'I know—I know! I can't very well pack up and leave her now, can I? So it looks as if I will have to stay after all.'

James shook his head. 'That wasn't what I meant at all, Penny. I'm sorry that this has happened, just when you needed to be free to make your choices. Look—it's late, and you're worn out. I'll leave you to get some sleep. I really shouldn't have called at this time of night, but I was anxious to know how Margaret was getting on.'

He turned to open the front door, but she reached out and grasped his arm. 'James, thank you for coming. I know I sound snappy, but I really do appreciate. . .' Her voice broke off as suddenly she was overcome by tears which seemed to spring from nowhere.

In an instant she was enclosed in a pair of strong, warm arms. She rested her head against James's chest as he held her tightly, whispering soothingly to her and gently ruffling her hair with his fingers.

At last she struggled from his arms, pushing him away slightly as she desperately tried to grasp the remnants of her dignity. 'How ridiculous,' she muttered, grabbing a handful of tissues from a box on the hall table and wiping her tear-stained face. 'You must think I'm a dreadful liability!'

James shook his head, reaching out to gently cup her

chin in his hand, turning her face so that he could look into her hollow, exhausted eyes.

'What I do think is that you need to look after yourself, or you'll be ill as well. Go to bed—get some sleep. Don't worry about coming in tomorrow—we'll manage. Goodnight, Penny.

He bent forward and briefly kissed her cheek. A moment later he was gone. Penny locked the door behind him, and then, turning, wearily leaned her back against it, too tired to move. She closed her eyes, and felt again those comforting arms around her. It was no good, she thought, shaking her head sadly. She had so little willpower—her resolve to put some distance between herself and James had crumbled so easily.

CHAPTER NINE

DESPITE her exhaustion, Penny was awake early the next morning, worrying about her grandmother's condition. The hospital hadn't telephoned, so presumably she had not deteriorated during the night, but Penny was anxious to see for herself, and after a swift breakfast of tea and toast she set off in her car for Ellminster General.

She knew that visiting didn't start officially until midday, but from her own experience of nursing sick patients she guessed that she would probably be allowed in. She was right—the staff nurse was quite happy to let her sit in with Margaret, who was in a single room opposite the nurses' station.

'Gran, it's Penny.' She took her grandmother's dry hand and held it tightly. The old lady's eyes opened almost immediately, and Penny was pleased to see instant recognition. Margaret was still wearing an oxygen mask, and looked weak and weary, but Penny could tell that she was already improving.

She sat beside the bed for most of the day, chatting while Margaret was awake, and reading during the frequent periods of sleep. At lunchtime Margaret was feeling strong enough to eat a little soup, and Penny's hopes began to rise.

'We'll probably move Mrs Lambert into the four-bedder this evening,' said the staff nurse when she came in to give the two o'clock antibiotics. 'She's doing so well.'

Penny nodded, pleased at the news. She knew that the

single rooms were usually kept for the very sick patients, or those needing isolation for any reason. To be moved out to the main ward was a good sign.

'I'll be going back to work tomorrow,' she said later, kissing her grandmother goodbye. 'I'll see you at lunchtime, and in the evening. Now behave yourself!'

She had a full waiting-room the following morning—several patients had waited a day to see her—and she was glad to lose herself in her work. The morning flew past in a whirl of blood tests, dressing changes, vaccinations and other minor treatments, and before she knew where she was it was twelve-thirty and she was free to go to lunch. There was some shopping she wanted to do for her grandmother, and then she could drop into the hospital for a few minutes before her afternoon clinic began. She was climbing into her car when James appeared beside her.

'Penny! Glad I caught you. . .' He looked more handsome than ever this morning, with freshly cut hair and a lightweight suit instead of his more usual sports jacket. 'How's Margaret?'

Briefly Penny outlined the situation, and he nodded his approval. 'Wonderful! I'm delighted. Give her my regards when you see her—tell her she's got to get back on her feet before the end of the cricket season. No one provides a cricket tea like Margaret Lambert!'

Penny laughed. 'I'll pass the message on—it's sure to do the trick. Gran's always open to a bit of flattery!'

'Good. Right—I'm off on my half-day now. What are you doing this weekend—I hope you're not going to be too lonely in that cottage by yourself?'

Penny shrugged. 'I've nothing planned apart from visiting Gran, but I don't get lonely. I've never minded my own company.'

James looked concerned. 'Listen, Penny—don't spend

tomorrow evening alone. Come and have supper with me. No strings, I promise—just as friends. I've got a surprise for you—something I think you'll enjoy.'

It was Penny's turn to frown. 'A surprise? Oh, I don't know. . . I suppose——' Her face cleared, and she smiled. 'Thank you, James. I'd like to come, but on one condition. . .'

'Which is. . .?'

'That I don't have to cook!'

He laughed. 'I promise—no cooking! That's all taken care of.'

He watched her drive away, glad she had accepted. He knew that the 'surprise' he had for her might take her away from him forever, but that was a risk he was going to have to run.

By Saturday evening Penny was in a cheerful mood. Margaret was making such a speedy recovery that there was talk of her coming home by the middle of the week, and this afternoon she had walked down the ward to sit in the day space with Penny, watching television.

'Hello!' Penny greeted James with a broad smile as he flung open the front door of his house. 'I'm not too early, am I? Here—I've brought some wine, and I just couldn't resist these! Can you use them?' She thrust a punnet of luscious-looking early strawberries into his hands, and followed him into the living-room.

James couldn't resist a wicked smile as he took in her appearance. 'It's a good thing the patients can't see you like that—I hate to think just what might happen to their blood pressures!'

'Oh, do you think it's too—um. . .' Penny looked down at herself. She had abandoned her favourite jeans and voluminous T-shirt in favour of a short, rather figure-hugging skirt and a silky top in a simple tunic style. Admittedly, she was showing quite a lot of leg, and she blushed, wondering if she had gone a bit over the top. James could be somewhat strait-laced sometimes. . .

'Not at all—you look fantastic! Now for the surprise I promised you. Come and meet the cook!'

He pulled her towards the kitchen, where a clattering of pans announced someone hard at work.

'We've got strawberries to add to your menu, Kit,' called James, standing in the doorway and blocking Penny's view of the kitchen. 'Come out and meet our guest—may I introduce Penny Lambert—my brother, Christopher Freeman.'

He stood back, and Penny's heart started to pound in her chest. Chris stood facing her, a smile already beginning to freeze on his lips. He had a vegetable knife in his hand and a tea-towel slung over his shoulder, and seemed as rooted to the spot as she was herself.

A moment's awkward silence was brought to an end by Chris. He blinked, widened his smile, and took a step forward. 'Penny—lovely to see you again! You used to staff on Monty's ward, didn't you? I've been trying to place you from James's description, but now, of course, I recognise you straight away!'

Penny wasn't sure she would be able to utter a sound, and felt curiously surprised to hear her own voice. 'Hello, Chris. This is the last place I'd have expected to run into you! Are you staying long?'

'Just for the weekend. I've dumped myself on my brother at short notice, as usual.'

James was busy pouring drinks, and now handed Penny a glass of wine which she was strongly tempted to gulp down in one go. She noticed that her hand was shaking slightly as she took the glass, but James didn't seem to spot anything amiss.

'Yes,' he said, directing her to the armchair and sitting himself down on the floor, 'as soon as I heard that Kit was coming down, I thought it would be a great opportunity for you to catch up with all the news from the Western—I always get the feeling that you miss the bright lights more than you admit.'

His tone was light-hearted, and he gave her hand a playful tweak, but the words were serious enough. Penny's mind was racing—did James really not know of the connection between his two guests? Chris was watching her, and she was careful not to meet his eye. She didn't want to give anything away.

The evening stretched ahead interminably. How was she going to get through three or four hours of conversation without revealing the fact that she was the woman James despised so much? And Chris? Was this all some sort of game to him, or did he want to keep their association secret just as much as she did? She didn't trust Chris Freeman—or Kit, as his family obviously called him—she didn't trust him one little bit.

'Are you still at the Western?' she asked politely, still not quite meeting his eye.

'Yes—but I'm just starting a leave of absence. I don't know how long I'll be away.'

'Oh, are you doing research, or something?'

'No, I'm taking time off for personal reasons. I'm not sure at the moment whether I'll be going back at all.'

'Oh.' What did that mean? No one volunteered any further details, and Penny searched her blank mind for something else to chat about.

James flung in one or two topics, but it must have been obvious that Penny and Chris were not at ease with one another. At least, Penny hoped it *wasn't* too obvious, but James was pretty sensitive, and it worried her that he would pick up their restraint.

He seemed cheerful enough, and after a while jumped up to check on the meal. Chris also rose from his chair, but James pushed him down again. 'No, no, I'll do it. You two must have a lot to talk about. If I need expert help I'll yell!'

Alone, Penny and Chris regarded each other with dismay. 'What the hell are you doing here?' gritted Penny between clenched teeth.

Chris looked amused at her discomfort. 'I might well ask you the same thing! I've been looking for you everywhere—if I'd known this was where you were hiding, I'd have been down to fetch you long ago!'

'What do you mean, *fetch*? I'm not some object you can pick up and put down! I left London to get away from you, and now you have to damned well turn up——'

'In case you're wondering, my brother hasn't a clue about our affair,' Chris put in. 'He innocently believes that he's brought us together for a good long yarn about the old days. . .makes you laugh, doesn't it?'

'It doesn't make *me* laugh.' Penny was careful to keep her voice down, aware of James clattering about in the little kitchen, but what her words lacked in volume she made up for by glowering at the smooth-talking doctor sitting opposite her.

'Don't frown like that, darling—it doesn't suit you.' After his initial surprise, Chris seemed to be rather enjoying this dangerous situation, and Penny despised him for it.

'I'm not your darling, and I just want to get out of this house tonight without James realising there's anything wrong.' She dropped her voice even further. 'I never wanted to see you again, and I hope after this evening I never do!'

Chris made a face at her just as James rejoined them from the kitchen.

'Perhaps the master chef could just cast his experienced eye over the cuisine, and then I think we can eat. Penny, another glass of wine?'

She put her hand over the glass. 'No, thanks, James—I'm driving.' More to the point, she thought, I've got to keep my wits about me during this horrible meal, otherwise I'm going to say something stupid and give myself away. So she hung on to the wine in her glass, and hoped that Chris might do the same.

It was a vain hope. As they sat down to their meal, Chris replenished his glass and gave her a benign smile across the table. Penny's spirits sank even further.

For James's sake she tried to keep up a normal, cheerful chatter, but it was probably the hardest thing she had ever done. Fortunately James was in high spirits himself, and he kept things rolling along almost singlehandedly.

'So,' he asked, holding up his glass in a toast to his guests, 'have you been catching up on old times, Penny? Is Kit tempting you back to city life?'

'Not at all—in fact, hearing about the *old days* in London only makes me more glad I left when I did!' Penny's remark was aimed specifically at Chris, and she hoped its meaning wasn't wasted.

James frowned a little at her acid tone, and glanced across at his brother. Careful, Penny warned herself, you're treading dangerously. . .

'Why *did* you leave the Western, Penny?' asked Chris wickedly.

She pursed her lips. 'For personal reasons—I'd rather not go into details, if you don't mind.'

'Ah!' Chris nodded seriously. 'I see—you don't want to discuss such matters with a virtual stranger. Well, I can't blame you for that. Anyway, I expect James has already heard the story.'

'No, as a matter of fact I know nothing about Penny's life in London,' said James. 'She's a very private person.'

Both men were watching her now, and Penny's cheeks grew hot. Chris was despicable—he was manipulating the conversation, teasing and tempting her into giving herself away. Well, she wasn't going to let him humiliate her without putting up a fight!

'OK, James—perhaps it's time I did open up a bit,' she admitted. 'I left London because of a man—as I'm sure you've already guessed. He treated me very badly— he was a liar and a cheat, and made my life so unbearable that in the end the only thing I could do was leave. Because of that one man I had to give up my job, my friends, my home. . .but that was the only way I could rid myself of him!'

There was a moment's stunned silence. Across the table Chris glowered at her, his face dark with anger. James was watching her closely, his eyes filled with pain. 'The bastard!' he whispered under his breath.

'Would you like to tell us his name?' growled Chris, his lips set in a thin line.

'I don't think that's necessary, do you?' Penny felt strangely calm, as if she had been relieved of a massive problem. 'This is wonderful, Kit!' She indicated the paella on her plate. 'How come you're such a good cook when James is so hopeless?'

James laughed, but Chris merely continued to scowl. 'James isn't quite as helpless as he likes to make out— it's an affectation. He pretends to be totally undomesticated so that women will want to look after him. It never fails.'

'Please excuse my brother,' said James with a deep

chuckle, 'he's suffering from acute self-pity at the moment.'

'Yes,' said Chris. 'My marriage, as I'm sure James will have told you, is on the rocks. My wife has thrown me out of my house—she won't even let me see my baby daughter. And all because of——'

'James told me,' interrupted Penny, suspecting that Chris was mad enough, or drunk enough, to throw away all caution and land them both in trouble. 'I'm sorry things have worked out so badly for you. Do you think you'll get back together with your wife?'

Chris gave her a sharp, questioning look. 'I don't know,' he said simply, shaking his head. 'I just don't know.'

James was clearing their plates and bringing in cheese and fruit, including Penny's strawberries. 'Let's change the subject—I'm sure Penny doesn't want to hear all your marital problems, Kit. Tell us what's going on in the smoke—have you been to the theatre recently? That's what's lacking in this part of the world. . .'

They discussed plays, and books, without much animation on the part of either Penny or Chris. Even James's enthusiasm seemed to flag after a while. He looked disappointed with his guests—the evening had not gone the way he had hoped. Something was wrong, but he couldn't quite make out what it was.

They finished the fruit, and with a look of relief James escaped into the kitchen to start making coffee.

'Sure you don't want me to do it?' teased Penny, only half joking—she would have welcomed the chance to avoid being left with Chris.

'No—I'm going to put paid once and for all to the rumours that I can't even boil a kettle!' James chuckled.

Alone, Chris and Penny sat in silence. She kept her eyes lowered, aware of his gaze boring into her, until she

could bear it no longer. She jumped up from the table
and crossed to an armchair, picking up the newspaper
that lay beside it and pretending to study the front page.
Suddenly the paper was wrenched from her hand, and
strong fingers clamped themselves around her wrist,
pulling her painfully to her feet.

'You must think you're a clever little bitch!' Chris
hissed at her, just loudly enough for her to hear, but not
so loud as to attract James's attention. 'You don't give a
damn, do you, that you've ruined my life—you just sit
there, telling me I treated you badly! What are you going
to do now—seduce my brother, if you haven't already?'

'Chris, let go! You're hurting me. . .'

'Ssh! If James hears you you're going to have a bit of
explaining to do. He's not stupid—and I don't think
he'd like to think he's been employing my ex-mistress in
his surgery. . .'

'Anyone for a brandy?' James called from the kitchen.
A moment later he appeared in the doorway bearing a
tray loaded with coffee-cups and a steaming jug of coffee.
Penny and Chris stood a few feet apart, Penny rubbing
her wrist where Chris's fingers had left an angry imprint
on her skin.

'Everything all right?' James frowned, looking from
one to the other.

'Fine!' Penny and Chris spoke simultaneously, each
smiling politely at their host, but avoiding one another's
eyes.

James continued to look puzzled, but said nothing,
obviously thinking that whatever the problem was, it
was best left alone. Penny sat down, making sure that
James was between herself and Chris. Shocked by the
sudden display of ill-will, she was determined not to find
herself alone with Chris again. Even with James present

she was distrustful. She knew he was playing some sort of game, but she didn't know the rules.

'Penny was just telling me how much she enjoys working with you, James,' drawled Chris in his smooth-as-silk voice. Penny cringed. The lie didn't surprise her—she was beginning to realise that Chris would stoop to any depths to pay her back for running away from him.

'I'm pleased to hear it.' James smiled at her. 'You can be such a fierce little thing that sometimes it's difficult to tell. Does this mean you've made up your mind about staying?'

'What's this about?' Chris looked interested.

'Neil and I are desperately trying to persuade Penny to accept a permanent contract,' James explained. 'We're lucky to have found her, and I for one don't intend to let her go easily.'

'Would you stop talking about me as if I wasn't here!' snapped Penny.

'Sorry!' James grinned, showing no remorse. 'But seriously, Penny, has talking to Kit this evening tempted you back to the excitement of a teaching hospital?'

'I don't think *Kit* could tempt me into anything!' retorted Penny.

Both men looked taken aback. Chris regained his composure. 'What makes you think I'd try, darling?'

Throwing away all caution, Penny rose to the bait. 'Because men like you never stop trying, Chris. You go on and on until you've got what you want. Well, that's not going to work with me any more!'

There was complete silence for a few minutes. Slowly James rose to his feet, and folded his arms. 'Would someone like to tell me what's going on?' His voice was ominously quiet.

Chris and Penny stared at one another, each silently

challenging the other to speak. At last Penny drew a deep breath.

'Yes, I will. I'm sick of this whole thing, anyway.' She looked up at James, meeting his eyes with a show of bravado. 'If you haven't already guessed, I'll enlighten you. I'm the nurse your brother had an affair with—the one who broke up his family—the one you despise!'

James gazed at her in consternation, his eyes showing a moment of wild emotion before he seemed to pull a steely shutter across his features. Faced with this hardness, Penny's will finally broke, and she lowered her eyes.

One word fell into the silence, and echoed around the room. 'You!'

'You!' repeated James, his eyes narrowed. 'All this time, it was you, and you didn't say a word!'

Suddenly Penny could see it all from his point of view—he had told her about the affair, the marriage break-up, and she had kept quiet, hiding her identity from him in a manner which must now seem to him to be deliberate and underhand.

'James, please let me explain. . . I. . .'

'There's nothing you need to say to me. I think you'd better go, don't you?' He was glaring at her. She couldn't believe her ears—he was throwing her out of his house!

He was breathing heavily, his lips compressed, the line of his jaw hard and unforgiving. Penny gazed helplessly at him, at a loss to know how to unravel this mess, how to put everything right between them. Because now, at this black moment, she realised just how much she *did* want things to be right. . .

She had one last try. 'James, can't we sit down and discuss this——'

'Like adults? Is that what you were going to say?' he interrupted. 'Like grown-up, sensible people? I can't see anything adult or sensible about the way you've behaved, Penny. You're clever—I'll grant you that. You fooled me completely, but now that's all over. I think the best thing is for you to go home, don't you?'

His voice was chillingly calm. As he spoke he was shepherding her towards the door, and before she knew what was happening she was outside on the pavement, clutching her bag close to her chest. She felt winded, as if someone had punched her in the chest.

For a few moments she could do nothing but stand, shaking slightly, disorientated by the speed of events. At last she fumbled in her bag for her car keys, and climbed unsteadily into the driving seat. Somehow she got herself home to Fernhill, and lay on her bed, fully dressed, her mind numb.

She fell into an exhausted sleep and woke early the next morning, feeling dirty and crumpled. She spent a long time under the shower, trying to wash away her self-disgust. She hadn't even put up a fight! She knew she was the innocent party, but she had allowed James to label her guilty, and had done nothing to defend herself. How could she have been so weak?

Feeling more awake but no less miserable, she drove slowly through the rain towards the hospital, not realising until she was halfway to Ellminster that it was too early to visit Gran.

She stopped in a layby and wondered what to do. It was ten-thirty on a wet Sunday morning, and the day yawned emptily in front of her. Was it too early to visit Jan? She started up the engine—what the heck, she was already unpopular enough, she might as well take the risk of annoying Jan and Steven.

'Come in! How lovely. . .' The welcome she received from Steven gave her a tiny flicker of warmth. 'Jan's just getting dressed—we're a bit lazy on a Sunday, I'm afraid. She'll be down in a minute or two. Coffee?'

'Mm, thanks, Steven! I'm sorry to land on you unannounced like this——' She apologised for the third time since ringing the doorbell, and Steven gave her a quizzical look.

'I've told you, Penny, you're always welcome! You look a bit tired—is there anything wrong? Is it your grandmother? We heard that she'd been taken back into the General. . .'

Penny shook her head, trying to force a smile. 'No, Gran's fine. She's doing really well. I'm sort of on my way to see her. . .'

Her voice tailed off, just as Jan appeared in the kitchen doorway. She looked wonderful—her hair was damp from the shower, and her face, bare of make-up, glowed healthily. She beamed with delight to find Penny there, and leaned forward to kiss her friend's cheek.

'Jan, you look fantastic! You're blooming at last!' Penny smiled, and Jan proudly patted her growing bulge.

'Yes—finally I'm able to enjoy carrying this little fellow around. I'm determined to make the most of it now, before the really hard part begins!'

She drew Penny into the sitting-room, leaving Steven to follow with the coffee. 'Sit down. You look worn out—what's been happening?'

Penny sighed, wondering where to begin. Steven came in with a tray, which he set down on the coffee table, and she hesitated, noting with surprise that he had only brought two cups.

'If you ladies will excuse me, I've got a pile of accounts to sort out. It's a godsend having you here, Penny— otherwise Jan would expect *me* to entertain her!'

They laughed. 'He's not a bad lad—I'm very lucky.' Jan looked at Penny and pulled a face. 'Although,' she added, 'if you've come to talk about what I *think* you've come to talk about, perhaps we should have asked him to stay. He might have been able to enlighten us on that most mysterious thing—the male mind!'

Penny smiled wryly and shook her head. 'I must be very transparent,' she sighed.

'No more than most of us—but you do look desperately unhappy. Come on, start at the beginning.'

Once she started, it was easy—everything came spilling out. Jan sat, nodding and listening, while Penny talked and talked, reliving every horrible moment of the previous evening. At last she stopped, spent, and stared gloomily into the cold dregs of her coffee.

'Penny, don't do anything rash. It's a bad time to rush into decisions, when you're so upset. . .'

'But I have to give my answer about the job tomorrow—and how can I stay now, with James despising me. . .'

'All the same, if I were you, I'd ask Neil for more time to think.'

Penny shrugged slightly. 'Maybe. . .oh, no! I've just seen the time—I'm supposed to be visiting Gran. Jan——' she took her friend's hand and squeezed it tightly. 'I can't tell you how grateful I am for a sympathetic ear. You're probably sick of hearing about my problems. . .'

Jan shook her head, grinning. 'Don't be daft—I only wish I could be of more help, but I think this is something you've got to work out for yourself.'

'I know. Goodness, how could I have got myself into this mess?'

Penny pondered this question as she drove the short distance to the hospital. Her grandmother was still making progress but had less energy than the previous day, and Penny didn't stay for too long. Visitors could be tiring, she knew, and she had no wish to hinder Gran's recovery.

She dreaded Monday morning. It was raining again, as it had been doing for most of the past week. Her hands trembled as she drove to work, and she prayed that she would not have to bump into James before she had had a chance to speak to Neil.

She was partly in luck. Neil was going to be late, Angela told her, due to an early emergency. James would fill in for him until he arrived to take his surgery. Hearing this, Penny scuttled straight into the treatment-room, not wanting to meet James, who was apparently already in the building.

Two patients arrived early for routine blood tests, and then her phone rang. She picked it up with a sinking heart. James's voice on the other end was businesslike and impersonal, for which she was strangely grateful. 'Will you start a course of tetanus vaccinations for my patient, please, Sister? I'll send him through with his notes.'

Somehow, his use of the title 'Sister' was more chilling than any vitriolic outburst. Penny presumed the patient had still been in the room with him, and wondered what he would have said if he had been alone. No use speculating—no doubt she would find out soon enough.

He sent two more patients during the course of the morning. At eleven-thirty Penny opened her door to call her next patient, and from the corner of her eye saw James heading out of the front door on his calls. She breathed a sigh—at least he was out of the way for the rest of the morning! She relaxed, knowing that he had gone, and enjoyed the rest of her clinic. She always liked doing the leg ulcer dressings, which she usually booked in at the end of the morning, because it was a good time to chat to the patients. They came anything from once to three times a week, and as it usually took many weeks to heal the ulcers, she got to know all sorts of things about themselves and their families.

Mrs Moore, whose ulcer Penny had spotted during her first elderly assessment, was still coming every week for treatment. The ulcer was slowly getting smaller, and Penny was pleased with the response. That visit to Mr and Mrs Moore's house seemed to have taken place a lifetime ago instead of just a few short weeks.

The old couple had been staying in Bournemouth with their daughter, so the usual Friday appointment had been postponed until today, but Penny was pleased to see that no harm had been done by the delay in treatment. She was applying a bandage impregnated with a moist, healing paste, and the to-and-fro motion of the bandaging technique was soothing and satisfying.

'I can remember my mother having something similar on her leg!' commented Mrs Moore.

'Yes, it's quite an old-fashioned remedy, but still one of the most reliable ways of healing varicose ulcers,' Penny told her. 'Some respond very well to the modern dressings, some seem to be more suitable for the good old paste bandages!'

Mrs Moore smiled. 'I don't mind what you use as long as I can get this old leg better. I find it hard to sit still for long, Sister. I like to be busy all the time—my husband says I'm like a bee buzzing around him all the time!'

'How is your husband?' asked Penny, starting to cover the paste bandage with an elastic bandage for support.

'Well, actually, Sister, he hasn't been too well. I wanted him to make an appointment with young Dr James, but he wouldn't hear of it. Says it's just old age, and he'd be wasting the doctor's time. But I don't like the look of him some days—he gets so breathless. . .'

'Perhaps you can use a bit of gentle persuasion, Mrs Moore,' said Penny, straightening up. 'There—finished! I'll dress it again on Friday.'

'Thank you so much, Sister.' Mrs Moore shuffled into her shoe, and gathered up her shopping bags. 'I will try and get my husband to come down here. I don't want him laid up—we're such a couple of old crocks as it is!'

Penny checked that Mrs Moore had been her last patient, then began on the task of clearing up the mess she had managed to make during the morning. There were a few forms to be filled in for vaccinations, and she had noticed that the dressing packs and sachets of sterile saline were running low. She would have to order in some more urgently.

She was completing her notes when the door opened behind her, and she twisted round in her chair to see James standing in the doorway, wearing an ominously serious expression. 'Have you finished for the morning?' His voice was cold.

Penny nodded. 'Except for this mountain of paper-work!' she added, over-brightly. Her lips were dry, and her hands shook a little. She dreaded whatever outburst was about to follow.

'Good. I think we need to sort out one or two things, don't you?'

'Look, James, you didn't let me explain the other evening——' she began.

'Penny, you don't need to tell me anything—I've heard the whole thing from Kit. More than enough, in fact.' He was standing beside her desk now, glaring down at her, hands on hips.

She was irritated by his aggressive stance. Whatever he might have in mind, she had no intention of feeling threatened by him. Calmly she shuffled her notes into a pile and placed them neatly in the filing basket. 'I bet that made interesting listening—lurid tales of how I tempted him away from his wife, and encouraged him to sneak around behind her back while she was busy bearing him a child? Well, I'm really not interested in what you or your brother think of me, James. I don't want anything more to do with either of you. I'm leaving here as soon as Neil can find someone to cover for me, and in the meantime I intend to see as little of you as possible. I imagine that arrangement will suit you too, Dr Yorke?'

She looked up and met his blue eyes. He stared at her, quivering with anger. At last he breathed just one word. 'Admirably!'

CHAPTER TEN

WITH shaking hands Penny prepared for her baby immunisation clinic. The patients were not due to arrive for over an hour, but she needed to be doing something while she gathered her thoughts together.

She had no doubt that James had been about to give her her marching orders—and she was glad she had got in first. But at what cost? She felt as if a part of herself had been ripped away, leaving a raw, gaping hole. To tell James that she wanted nothing to do with him. . .it was so final, and so untrue.

Shuddering, she tried to mentally list the things she had to do now. First of all, she must speak to Neil. That was not going to be pleasant either. Then she would have to find out whether her mother would be back in England by the time her grandmother came out of hospital. Obviously she couldn't leave Gran on her own, but if her mother was around to help with her convalescence, then there was no need for Penny to stay. And, she thought sadly, the greater distance she could put between herself and James Yorke, the better.

With sinking heart she picked up the phone and buzzed Neil's extension. She half hoped he would still be out on his calls, but after a few moments his mild, friendly voice answered, and told her that yes, of course she could come and talk to him. Right away.

He sat behind his desk, surrounded by his usual confusion of notes. Penny perched nervously on the patients' chair, her heart pounding.

'I—um. . .thank you, Neil, for offering me the permanent contract, but I'm afraid I can't accept the job. As soon as you can find someone to cover for me, I shall be leaving Ellminster.'

Neil looked devastated. He frowned at her, uncomprehending. 'Where are you going?' he asked.

Penny shook her head. 'I'm not sure. Back to London, I expect.'

'You mean you're just leaving, without another job to go to? But why—I suppose it's something to do with James, is it?'

'Yes. It's a long, complicated story, which I won't go into, but I really can't stay here. You were right all along—it was a mistake to get involved with a colleague. I wish I'd listened to you in the first place.'

Neil sighed, tapping his pen on the edge of the desk. 'I'm sorry to hear all this, Penny. I value the contribution you make to this practice. And I have to admit, I thought I'd been wrong to warn you about your relationship with James. I thought the two of you could work well together. Look——' he paused, leaning forward in his chair to gaze earnestly at her '—would it help if you had some time off? Try and sort things out with James, then perhaps you'd feel differently about staying. . . I'll leave the job offer open. . .'

'You're a kind man, Neil, but I'm afraid it's too late for any of that. In fact, if you can get an agency nurse to cover for me, I'd like to leave as soon as possible.'

'I'm sorry things have worked out this way, Penny. We'll miss you, and so will the patients.'

A lump rose in Penny's throat. 'Thank you,' she whispered, and hurried out of the door before Neil's sad face could reduce her to tears.

She felt drained, but there was work to be done. The immunisation clinic was busy but straightforward, and so was the evening surgery which followed. She threw herself into the work, and raced through, so that by five-thirty she had finished and tidied her room. She took her basket of notes out for Angela to file, and almost collided with a man striding away from the reception desk.

'Chris!' she exclaimed.

'Hello, Penny. I was just coming to see you.'

They stood facing one another in the busy reception area. Chris was not as tall as James, but still he seemed to tower over her. He looked down at her seriously, the brashness of Saturday night gone.

'Well—look, we can't really talk here. You'd better come through to my room. . .'

Flustered, she led the way to the treatment-room and shut the door behind him. In the middle of the room, he turned and faced her, a faintly apologetic smile hovering on his lips.

'I've come to say goodbye, Penny.'

'You're going back to London?' she queried.

'No. I've got leave of absence from the Western—I'm going over to the States to try and patch things up with Susie. I'm not sure if I'll succeed, but I'm going to have a damned good try!'

Penny hesitated, wondering how to take this new, serious Chris. Where was the teasing, bantering tone? The womaniser, the irresistible, egotistical charmer? Something had changed. He wasn't a man to be feared any more. 'I'm glad,' she said at last. 'I hope you manage to save your marriage. A wife and child—that's got to be worth fighting for!'

Chris nodded. 'I've had a lot of sense knocked into me in the last couple of days. My big brother decided it was time I grew up, and learnt a few home truths about myself. It was a painful process—one I wouldn't care to repeat.'

'Oh, dear—but you appear to have survived. . .'

Penny was still unsure how to take this apparent change of character. It seemed too sudden.

'Yes—what's the expression—"bent, but not broken". . . Listen, Penny, I'm on my way to the station now, but I couldn't leave without coming to see you, and apologising for everything that happened in London. I deceived you, and you deserved better than that. I don't suppose you'll ever forgive me, but I want you to know that I did care for you—very much. I knew damned well that you wouldn't have anything to do with me if you knew I was married, so I pretended I was single. And then, when you called it all off, I seemed to go completely mad. I couldn't think of anything except getting you back.'

'You ruined my life, Chris,' Penny said quietly. 'You shouldn't do that to people you care about.'

He ran a hand through his hair in a despairing gesture that reminded her sharply of James. Despite the fact that they were not actually related, they shared so much.

He glanced at his watch. 'I'd better get a taxi—James was going to run me to the station in Swindon, but apparently he's been called out. Can I use this phone?'

'I'll drive you.' The words were out before Penny had time to think.

'If it's not too much trouble. . .' Chris looked surprised.

'Of course not. At least that way I'll be sure you're on your way back to your family!'

The traffic was heavy, and they only just made it to the station in time for the London train. They spoke very little during the drive, except to exchange polite comments about the scenery, but Penny felt remarkably relaxed, as if she was reaching the end of a difficult journey, and a haven was in sight.

Chris seemed to share her feeling of finality. Standing

at the barrier, with the train waiting on the platform, doors agape, he smiled ruefully at her.

'It's over, Penny—I don't think there's anything I can do to make amends, except wish you happiness. Perhaps we'll meet again——'

'I doubt it,' retorted Penny, 'as I have no idea where I shall be in a few days' time.'

He opened his eyes wide in surprise. 'You're leaving after all?'

'Yes—I can't stay now. Thanks to our past—*escapades*—your brother can hardly bear the sight of me.'

'Is that what he says?'

'Not in so many words, but it's obvious just how low his opinion of me is.'

'And does his opinion matter that much to you?'

'Yes, of course it does!' shouted Penny, and then, realising that she was revealing too much, she bowed her head.

Chris gave a soft whistle. 'You're in love with him, aren't you?' Unable to deny it, Penny said nothing. 'He always had all the luck,' muttered Chris.

The whistle blew. Suddenly he leaned forward and hugged her warmly, planting a kiss on her cheek. 'Goodbye,' he whispered.

Penny suddenly found her voice. 'Chris! Please—do one last thing for me. . .'

He nodded, a questioning expression on his face.

She took a deep breath, and spoke through clenched teeth. '*Don't say a word to James!*'

She watched the train pull out, then turned, hands in her pockets, to find James standing a few feet behind her.

'Very touching!' The chill of his tone made her shiver.

'What are you doing here?' she asked, frowning.

'I thought I'd come and see my brother off, but I found someone had beaten me to it!'

'You were out on call—I offered to drive him. . .' she began.

'How convenient!'

She was struggling to make sense of all this. 'James, surely you don't think. . .'

'I know what I saw, Penny. Don't give me any more of that rubbish about Kit making your life miserable— the way you two said your farewells seemed to suggest otherwise.'

'How dare you—you overbearing——' Desperately Penny searched around for a fitting description, but before she could come out with anything James laughed.

'Save your breath. I don't think I'm going to be too upset by the kind of insults you can think up! I've heard a lot worse, believe me!'

She clamped her lips together, breathing heavily. This man was completely impossible!

'I'm going home.' Thrusting her hands more deeply into her jacket pockets, she turned away and began marching towards the car park.

Footsteps followed her, and in a couple of strides James was back at her side. 'I just want to know one thing, Penny——'

She wheeled round and confronted him, her small face turned up to his, the colour high in her cheeks.

'What is it?' she snapped.

'How long did you think you could keep your affair with Kit a secret from me? Would you ever have told me if he hadn't turned up at my house?'

Penny shook her heard wearily. 'I don't know,' she replied honestly. 'I guessed how you'd react—and I was right. I knew you'd take your brother's side against me. It's hardly worth wasting my breath trying to tell my side of the story. You're brothers, and you're going to stick together, aren't you? I suppose it's only to be expected. . .'

Sadly she turned away and walked the few yards to her car. As she drove off she noticed in her rear-view mirror that James was still standing on the same spot, watching her moving away from him in the direction of Ellminster.

Passing through reception the following morning, Penny was surprised to see Mr and Mrs Moore sitting in the waiting area. Noticing her, Mrs Moore gave a little wave and beckoned her over.

'He wasn't well when I got back yesterday, Sister. I managed to get him an appointment for this morning, and for once he didn't argue!' She pulled a knowing expression and cocked her head slightly towards her husband, who sat leaning forward in his chair, breathing rather noisily.

Penny frowned a little. He looked more suitable for a home visit than to be sitting here in the crowded surgery. 'You haven't walked here, have you?' she asked, watching the elderly man pursing his lips as he exhaled.

'No, Sister—we came in a taxi, and the driver's coming back for us later.'

'Good. Well, I hope you don't have to wait too long.'

Thoughtfully Penny returned to her room to start her clinic. She hadn't liked the look of Mr Moore—his skin had an unhealthy grey pallor, and he hadn't seemed aware of anything going on around him.

Her first patient needed a support bandage for a sprained ankle. The second was a child with swollen glands in her neck, which the mother thought might be mumps. Penny didn't think so, and referred them back to Neil for his opinion. Her third patient was a middle-aged man who had had a large mole removed from his back. The histology report confirmed that the mole was quite harmless, and Penny explained this to him while she prepared to take out the two stitches from the biopsy site.

She was swabbing the skin with saline when the telephone rang—James's extension light flashed.

'I need you in here now with the resus bag!'

James's tone left no room for doubt. 'I'm sorry, Mr Holland—there's an emergency. . .' Penny grabbed the resuscitation bag which was always kept by the door, and ran out of the room, leaving her bewildered patient sitting on the couch, stripped to the waist.

This was the first time any kind of emergency had occurred in the surgery since Penny had started work here, and her adrenalin surged as she burst into James's room. In one glance she took in the scene—the patient's chair overturned beside the desk—James kneeling over the prone figure of Mr Moore, listening anxiously with his stethoscope to the patient's chest.

'We'll need oxygen—and have an airway ready just in case. . .'

Penny ran back into the corridor to fetch the portable oxygen cylinder which was kept on a shelf midway between the doctors' rooms. In a moment she was connecting it to a clean mask, and James slipped it over Mr Moore's face.

'He's breathing, and he's got an irregular pulse. Call an ambulance! I just hope we can keep him stable until it gets here. . .'

He checked Mr Moore's blood pressure while Penny rang for an ambulance.

'They're on their way,' she said, kneeling beside him. 'What do you think it is—coronary?'

He shook his head. 'I think it could be a pulmonary

embolism. Look at the veins in his neck—they're pulsating. His BP's in his boots and he's got a pleural rub. From what he was telling me before he collapsed it sounds as if he's had a series of little clots in the lungs over the past few days.'

'You know his wife is waiting outside?'

James groaned. 'One of us had better speak to her before the ambulance arrives. I'll go—you stay here and keep a check on his pulse and BP.'

With a pounding heart Penny knelt beside the semi-conscious figure, and gently smoothed a strand of white hair away from his forehead. His breathing was very laboured, despite the oxygen. She knew that a clot on the lung could be rapidly fatal, and prayed that the old man would hang on until they could get him into hospital for treatment.

The pulse was so feeble that once or twice she thought it had stopped. She grabbed the stethoscope and listened to the heart, hearing the irregular beats with relief. 'Don't worry, Mr Moore,' she said, unsure whether the poor man could hear her or not, 'you'll be in hospital in no time. You'll soon be feeling more comfortable.' She checked the blood-pressure, which was low but stable, and carried on talking, repeating the reassuring words, as much for her own benefit as for the patient's. Come on, come on, she said to herself, where's the ambulance? Where's James?'

The door opened and James reappeared, closely followed by two ambulance crew, one wearing a paramedic's jacket. Swiftly they went to work, transferring Mr Moore to a trolley and connecting him up to their own portable oxygen supply. Penny reported her latest blood-pressure and pulse readings.

'I think he'd better have a line up now—you might have to get some fluid into him if his BP drops any more,' said James. The paramedic nodded his agreement, and produced an intravenous line and cannula. Quickly James inserted a needle into the vein in Mr Moore's arm, and the line was connected up, with an infusion of fluid running slowly to keep the vein open.

'OK, off we go!' The ambulance crew manoeuvred the trolley out of the cramped surgery, and started off at speed towards the rear entrance, thus avoiding the reception area. Mrs Moore was waiting to accompany her husband to the hospital, and Penny put an arm around her shoulders as she walked with her out to the car park and the waiting ambulance.

'Oh, Sister, is he going to be all right?' Mrs Moore was dabbing her eyes with a handkerchief.

Penny wished she knew the answer. 'I hope so, Mrs Moore,' she replied honestly. 'They'll do everything they can for him at the hospital.'

'It's my fault, Sister—I knew he wasn't right, and I should have made him come to the doctor before. . .'

'Don't blame yourself—it's no one's fault. These things just happen out of the blue. It was just as well that it happened here, with the doctor on hand.'

They had reached the ambulance, and the paramedic helped Mrs Moore inside and gave her a seat beside her husband, where she could sit and hold his hand.

Penny saw them off, and returned inside. Suddenly she remembered that she had left a patient halfway through removal of stitches, what seemed like hours ago. She glanced at her watch as she hurried to the treatment-room, and saw with surprise that the whole episode had taken less than fifteen minutes.

Mr Holland was nowhere to be seen. Penny's dressing trolley was just as she had left it, but the room was empty. She looked outside in the waiting space, but only two patients were sitting there, and neither was the one she sought.

She started off down the corridor towards reception, and met Angela coming the other way. 'If you're looking for Mr Holland, he's gone,' she said. 'He said he didn't know how long you'd be, and he had another appointment to get to. He's coming back this evening.'

'Oh—OK. Thanks, Angela.'

With a sigh, Penny returned to clear her trolley and prepare for the next patient. Excitement over, time to get back to the routine, inevitable ear syringing!

She was tired by the time she had shut the door on the last patient—physically and emotionally drained. So much seemed to have happened over the past few days, it was difficult to keep track of it all. Her whole personal life had been turned upside down, and now—poor Mr Moore!

She was thinking about him, wondering how he was getting on, when there was a tap at her door. James put his head round. 'Penny—bad news, I'm afraid. Mr Moore died soon after arriving at the General.'

It was the final straw. Penny sank down at her desk, put her head on her arms, and let the tears flow. She had seen death many times during her career as a nurse, but seldom had she felt quite as devastated as she did now.

A voice murmured softly in her ear, and a hand stroked her hair as she sobbed quietly. At last she looked up to find James perched on the edge of her desk, watching her tenderly. This sudden show of concern wasn't what she wanted, and furiously she grabbed a handful of tissues from the box in front of her and scrubbed at her eyes.

'You must be getting fed up with seeing me in tears,' she muttered.

'Everyone's entitled to cry for the people they care about.'

'Did you find out what happened?' she asked.

'Not in any detail, but as far as I can gather he deteriorated in the ambulance, and arrested in the emergency-room. It must have been a massive embolism.'

Penny sighed. 'I've nursed a lot of dying patients over the years, but it's amazing since I came here how quickly I've grown used to helping people stay well. It came as a shock to be face to face with an acutely ill patient again.'

'Which kind of nursing do you prefer?' asked James.

Penny didn't hesitate. 'This kind. Preventative medicine—health education. It's so fundamental, isn't it?'

'I agree, of course, otherwise I wouldn't be a GP. Some people thrive on the acute side, though, don't they? Mr brother, for instance. He'd probably die of boredom in general practice—he's at his happiest with a scalpel in his hand!'

The mention of Chris jolted Penny's memory. 'I suppose he's in America by now—back with his wife and child.'

James looked at his watch. 'No, not yet. He'll still be on the aircraft.'

She frowned. 'But wasn't he flying out last night?'

'No.' He shook his head. 'He was staying with a friend near Heathrow. He had an early flight this morning. I thought you would have known all this.'

'Why? What reason could he have for telling me his itinerary? Next you'll be telling me how surprised you are that I didn't spend the night with him last night!'

James fixed her with a cold look. 'Now you're getting hysterical! Let's change the subject—talk about anything but my fool of a stepbrother! Have we got everything we need for tomorrow's diabetic clinic?'

Penny groaned and clapped her hand to her forehead.

'Penny! You haven't forgotten that we've invited our first batch of patients to tomorrow afternoon's clinic?'

'No, of course not. Don't worry, James—I'll make sure your clinic runs like clockwork. I don't know who'll be helping you with next month's session, though. I shall be long gone by then, you'll be pleased to hear.'

'Let's just get tomorrow safely out of the way, shall we? I'll worry about next month when I have to.'

With that he left. Penny shut her eyes, which still stung from the tears she had shed for Mr Moore. James didn't care about her leaving—all that talk of being fond of her, of wanting her to stay—it had all been a sham. Now he couldn't wait for her to get out of the way so that he could forget that she had ever existed.

How long could she bear to stay here? She hoped Neil would be able to find someone to cover for her soon. Working alongside James every day was quickly becoming unbearable. Fortunately it was Neil's turn to take the well woman clinic this afternoon, but tomorrow was James's baby, the diabetic clinic, and she certainly couldn't let him down over that. But after tomorrow. . . she would have to jog Neil's arm and remind him that she wanted to leave as soon as possible.

In the hospital that evening Penny handed her grandmother a letter which had arrived in the morning post. She smiled as she watched Margaret scan the familiar handwriting on blue airmail paper.

'Excellent news, isn't it, Gran? Mother's handed over her job—she'll be here on Friday!'

'And I've got some more good news—they're letting me out on Saturday, if I behave myself.' Margaret smiled.

'Oh, fantastic! It's going to be a marvellous weekend, having both you and Mother at home together!' Penny hugged her grandmother warmly, and sat beside the bed, holding the old lady's hand.

'Now,' said Margaret firmly, 'you can tell me exactly what's been going on. I know you've been going through some sort of crisis, and I've been lying here worrying about what it could be. Now that I'm on the mend, perhaps you'd like to enlighten me?'

Penny looked reluctant. Margaret shook her head and clicked her tongue in exasperation. 'The only thing I'm sure of is that James Yorke is somewhere at the bottom of it. I do hope that young man isn't going to hurt you. Perhaps I should have a word with him. . .'

'No, Gran, you mustn't——' Penny had reacted before she noticed the wicked gleam in the old lady's eye. 'You're impossible, Gran! You're such a schemer— very well, I'll tell you what's been happening. It isn't a very pretty story, I warn you. . .'

She delivered a 'tidied-up' version of the sorry tale, and Margaret for once kept quiet to the end, nodding her head wisely from time to time. At the end she let out a long sigh. 'Well, you're not the first young woman to be taken in by a married man, and I'm sure you won't be the last. But it strikes me that you haven't opened up enough to James—you haven't *talked* to him.'

'I've tried, Gran, but he's determined not to listen. He's already made his judgement, and I'm not going to crawl to him, begging him to give me another chance!'

'That pride of yours is going to be your downfall, Penny,' her grandmother cautioned.

'Thanks for the warning! No, I think I must accept that I've made a complete and utter mess of this, and retire with a few shreds of self-respect intact. Once I get tomorrow's clinic over and done with, I'll be able to leave as soon as there's a replacement. I don't like letting people down, but the day I leave that surgery behind can't come soon enough!'

That wasn't true, Penny mused as she drove to work the following morning. It wasn't the practice she wanted to leave behind, but one particular GP. The work, the patients, the atmosphere—she would miss them all like mad.

Her first job that morning was to do a pregnancy test for a patient who had been trying to have a baby for three years. After two miscarriages Louise Palmer had waited anxiously for more than a year without becoming pregnant. Now she and her shy-looking husband stood in Penny's treatment-room, triumphantly holding the sample bottle.

Penny took it and looked at her watch. 'Do you want to come back later for the result?'

'Can we wait? Will you be able to do it straight away?'

'I don't see why not—I've no one else waiting yet. It'll take about ten minutes—all right?'

They nodded, smiling nervously, and still holding hands sat down outside in the waiting space.

Barely ten minutes later Penny ushered them back into her room. 'It's positive!' she said, smiling broadly. 'Congratulations!'

The delight of the couple was touching, and as they threw their arms around each other and hugged and kissed, Penny discreetly stepped out of the room. Their moment of joy needed to be spent in private. When she returned with a form to be signed by Louise, the couple had composed themselves, but the excitement kept bubbling through. Penny gave advice about consulting the doctor, and wished them luck.

'Thank you, Sister,' cried Louise, shaking her by the hand as she left. 'You've no idea how much this means to us!' They left, Mr Palmer's arm protectively around his wife's waist, and Penny felt a pang of something—envy? Suddenly she felt very alone. She had no one with whom to share hopes and joys, or even sorrows. No one to protect her, cherish her, be there for her. . . Stop it! she told herself. You're getting maudlin.

After the Palmers, she took two blood tests and gave dietary advice to an eighteen-stone man who had just been to see Neil about his high blood-pressure. She spent a little while explaining how shedding some weight would help to reduce his blood-pressure to a safer level, and then asked him about the kind of food he ate. Finally she asked him to keep a diary of everything he consumed for a fortnight, and to come back and see her then.

'A challenge' was how Neil referred to the seriously overweight patients, and certainly this one was going to be just that. From what he had told her, John Monkton lived on salad and crispbread, but Penny had serious doubts about that, and looked forward to seeing his diary. It should make interesting reading! A good hour later it hit her in a blinding flash that she probably wouldn't be *here* when Mr Monkton returned in two weeks' time. 'Oh, no!' she said aloud, dismayed at the idea. Leaving the practice was going to be more of a wrench than she had thought!

CHAPTER ELEVEN

'OK, MAUREEN, would you like to show me how you test your blood at home?' Penny was enjoying herself. Seventeen-year-old Maureen was the third diabetic patient that afternoon, and all Penny's knowledge and counselling skills were coming back to her.

Maureen was, as she had suspected, rushing the blood test and not getting a very accurate result. Carefully Penny showed her how to use a watch to time the test from the moment the drop of blood came into contact with the reactive patch on the special plastic strip.

The urine testing seemed to be less of a problem, but as Penny looked through Maureen's record book she began to doubt whether the girl was really testing for sugar on a daily basis. The whole of the previous week's results had been filled in in the same black pen, raising the idea in Penny's mind that Maureen might have written them all down at once, possibly just before coming to the clinic.

'Tell me how you feel about having to do these tests every day,' she said, watching Maureen's reaction carefully. She knew from past experience that teenagers, having coped with their diabetes since perhaps as early as eight or nine years of age, often rebelled against the constraints of the condition.

'It's a drag,' admitted Maureen. 'If you must know, I hate it—it makes me angry. It's bad enough having to keep injecting insulin, and watching that I don't go hypo—but all that mucking about with urine tests and blood tests. . .' She bit her lip. 'They're usually all right, so sometimes I don't bother.'

'Maureen, if you don't do the tests, how are you going to know whether you've got good control?' asked Penny gently. She spent a few minutes explaining the importance of preventing future complications, and Maureen listened closely, nodding her understanding.

There were five patients booked into this afternoon's clinic, and Penny screened each one initially for general health, dietary problems, glucose monitoring and general advice and information. The specific help she offered varied from patient to patient. Some were relatively recently diagnosed, and were still learning how to cope with their condition, and others had lived with their diabetes for much of their lives. A few already had symptoms of complications such as visual and circulation problems, with which Penny was only too familiar after her years on Monty's ward at the Western.

After seeing Penny the patients went on to consult James, who checked that the dosage of medication or insulin was providing adequate control of the blood glucose levels, and adjusted them accordingly.

The two-hour session seemed to fly past. Penny was sorting out her notes, having sent the last patient through to see James, when the phone rang and Angela announced that Steven O'Connell was in reception and asking to see her.

'Send him through, Angela.' Penny's heart raced—surely nothing could have happened to Jan and her baby? After all this time, it would be too cruel. . .

Steven's smiling face dispelled this fear, but Penny was still puzzled by the reason for his call. After all, he and Jan were not patients at this practice.

'Sorry to interrupt you during working hours, Penny,' he began, 'but I wanted to have a word without Jan finding out. It's her birthday on Saturday, and I'd like to get some of our friends together for a bit of a party—and I want it to be a surprise.'

'Good idea—she'll love that!'

'Yes—poor old Jan, she's been through such a rough time recently. I've left it very late to arrange this, I know—please say you'll be able to come.'

The door opened and James appeared, hesitating in the doorway when he saw that Penny was not alone. 'Oh, sorry. . . Steven! How's Jan?'

'Just the chap I wanted to see. . . Jan's fine, thanks, James—in fact, she's so well I'm trying to rustle up a surprise party for her on Saturday. I was just pleading with Penny to drop everything else and come. It's short notice, I know, but it would be great if you could both be there. . .'

Penny hesitated. Much as she would like to celebrate her friend's birthday, she didn't want to do so in the company of James! 'I'm not sure, Steven. . .you see, my grandmother should be coming out of hospital on Saturday, and I——'

'Oh, of course—I understand. You won't want to leave her on her own. . .'

James frowned at Penny. 'Didn't you mention this morning that your mother was coming home on Friday?'

Penny remembered that she had shared her good news with everyone at coffee-time. 'Yes,' she said slowly, 'that's right, but——'

'So if you wanted to go to Jan's party, Margaret wouldn't be completely alone?'

Penny glared at him. Why was he interfering like this? 'Well, perhaps for an hour or so. . .' she said doubtfully.

Steven smiled. 'That would be great, Penny! How about you, James?'

'Sorry, I'm on call!'

Penny greeted this news with a sense of relief, but Steven groaned. 'Oh, no—bad luck! Jan's going to be disappointed.' He turned to Penny and adopted an expression of mock despair. 'It's all up to you, Penny—please don't let me down!'

She laughed. 'OK, Steven, I promise I'll be there!'

As the door closed behind Jan's husband, James wheeled round to confront Penny. 'You made that a bit obvious—you were only prepared to go to the party once you knew I was on call!'

'Don't be ridiculous—it doesn't make a jot of difference to me whether you're there or not!' Penny hadn't meant her reply to sound quite so abrasive, but the words were out and it was too late.

James narrowed his eyes. 'Is that right?' was all he said.

The next two days passed in a whirl as Penny prepared for the double homecoming. She rushed home from work on Thursday and cleaned the cottage from top to bottom, airing the spare bed for her mother and picking armfuls of flowers from the garden to fill every available vase.

After weeks of cool showery weather, summer had suddenly arrived with a vengeance, and the temperature soared. The blue skies and hot sunshine seemed to raise everyone's spirits, including Penny's. Ellminster took on a serene beauty in the clear June light, and even the market stalls on Friday morning looked more cheerful and colourful than ever.

Penny noticed Mrs Moore's name added to the end of her morning clinic, and as soon as the elderly woman came in she offered her condolences.

'Thank you, Sister. I know you and Dr Yorke did everything you could—you were wonderful. It's just a

mercy that it was all so quick. He had so many years of
pain with his arthritis—at least at the end he didn't
suffer for long.'

Penny swiftly changed the dressing on Mrs Moore's
leg, noticing that there were definite signs of improve-
ment. She pointed out the healthy new tissue to Mrs
Moore.

'Oh, that's good,' her patient replied, but there was
little interest in her voice. 'As long as this leg carries me
into the church for George's funeral on Monday, I'm not
bothered what happens after that.'

She was obviously feeling very low, and Penny
resolved to mention the fact to James. Perhaps he could
keep an eye on Mrs Moore over the next few weeks.

The day raced on, and at last it was time to drive to
the airport to meet her mother's flight.

'Darling!' Cries of delight and laughter mingled as the
two women stood hugging on the concourse, parting to
look at one another before embracing once again.
Josephine Lambert was an older, slightly taller version
of her daughter, with the same slight build and fair
colouring. Her hair was longer, though, caught up in an
unruly knot on the top of her head, and her eyes were
greener than Penny's. With three years to catch up on,
their excited chatter began immediately, and continued
almost non-stop throughout the drive back to Gloucestershire, and for the rest of the evening.

Josephine was thrilled to hear that her mother-in-law
would be home with them the following day. 'What
luck, that I was able to get home just in time! It'll be
lovely—the three of us together!'

Penny explained about Jan's birthday party in the
evening, and her mother waved her hands dismissively.
'Go—enjoy yourself, darling! Margaret and I are both
going to be in need of a quiet evening, anyway. I'm glad

you've got some social life—this isn't the most exciting place for young people. When your father and I were engaged, and he used to bring me here to stay with his parents, I thought the place was absolutely dead! I love it now, of course.'

Penny laughed. 'It's not that bad! Anyway, when I left London I needed somewhere like this—it was a kind of recuperation! And then I found it wasn't quite as restful as I'd thought. . .'

They talked long into the night, before falling into bed, exhausted.

Margaret Lambert was sitting in the day-room fully dressed, her suitcase beside her, when they arrived to collect her from the hospital at lunchtime the next day.

'You took your time!' she cried by way of a greeting. 'I've been ready since nine o'clock!' She was very scathing towards the staff nurse who suggested taking her down to the main entrance in a wheelchair, and, picking up her own case, strode out of the ward like a woman only half her age.

Almost helpless with laughter, Penny and her mother thanked the ward staff for their care before racing to catch up with the old lady, who was by now holding open the lift doors with her foot and waving at them impatiently.

Jan's party was due to start at eight-thirty. Penny took her time getting ready, enjoying the luxury of wallowing for ages in a hot bath. Afterwards, wrapped in a huge towel, she painted her nails carefully and sat by the open window looking out over the garden, waiting for the varnish to dry. The roses were opening, and the scent of the old-fashioned climber sprawling over the sitting-room window wafted up on the warm evening air. She closed her eyes and let out a contented sigh. Just for this evening she was going to forget about James, forget about her uncertain future, and enjoy the company of her friends!

With her nails dry, her hair brushed into a gleaming cap which framed her face, and a little make-up skilfully applied, she climbed into her dress.

There wasn't a lot to it. It was a simple style, in a rich coral colour which complemented her fair skin and hair. Sleeveless and straight, the respectable hemline sat just on Penny's knee. From the front it was quite a demure dress—it was the back which made it something different!

'How does that dress stay on, darling—willpower?' asked her mother, as Penny presented herself to them before setting off.

'It's more secure than it looks,' Penny reassured her. She knew the plunging neckline at the back was dramatic—that was why she liked it.

'You look wonderful—I hope he's worth it, whoever he is.'

'Thank you, but I'm going to this party alone. Now, behave yourselves, girls! Don't wait up.'

She picked up her bag and car keys, and left, knowing that as soon as the door closed behind her Gran would be launching into the whole story of her on-off, never-to-develop romance with James. Oh well, she thought, let them have a good gossip—I really don't care any more.

Jan had been warned about the party earlier that day—Steven didn't want to risk giving her too much of a shock. She was delighted to see everyone, and glided around her guests, smiling radiantly and carrying her growing bump in front of her like a trophy.

'Gosh, what a stunning dress!' she cried, walking all round Penny to admire the back view. 'I wonder if I'm ever going to get into anything like that again?' She patted her stomach with pretended ruefulness.

'Darling, you look splendid just the way you are,' said her husband, coming up to slide an arm around her waist.

Penny grinned at the happy pair and moved away to find herself a drink. Angela was on the other side of the room with her boyfriend, and as Penny waved at them she began to wonder if she was the only person at the party without a partner.

Angela was attacking the avocado dip with a breadstick when Penny arrived beside her. The boyfriend seemed to have disappeared.

'Is Neil coming tonight?' asked Penny, picking up a tiny sausage roll.

'No—he's on call,' replied Angela.

Penny froze, holding the sausage roll up to her lips. 'He can't be—James told me it was *his* weekend on call.'

Angela nodded. 'It was, but they swapped at the last minute. Neil's wife wanted him to go to some family get-together next weekend, so. . .'

She rambled on, but Penny wasn't listening. Suddenly she wasn't hungry any more, and put her plate down. Anxiously she look around the room for the familiar dark head, but there was no sign of James. She had no reason to suppose he would come, but somehow she just knew he would. She picked up her glass of mineral water and moved off restlessly to circle around the group of guests. What worried her more than anything was her own reaction to the possibility of seeing James tonight—why was she getting into this ridiculous state? Her stomach was churning, her mouth dry—when Steven came by with a bottle of white wine and peered into her empty glass, she allowed him to fill it up, not giving a thought to the necessity of driving herself home.

A few minutes later, her glass empty once again, she felt a bit better. There was still no sign of James—perhaps he wasn't coming after all. She began to relax and joined a chattering group of women who were discussing whether Jan should go in for a water birth when the time came.

Suddenly she felt a *frisson* down her back—she knew without turning round that James had come into the room. Perhaps she had caught the sound of his voice without realising—whatever it was, her bare arms were covered in goose-pimples, and her hands began to shake.

'James, you made it after all! How lovely—oh, is that for me? *Thank* you. . .' Jan's delighted voice rang out over all the chatter, and Penny forced herself to keep her back to the door.

'Penny, have another drink?' She hardly noticed who had spoken, but held out her glass obediently and gulped down a mouthful of wine.

The group was disintegrating, people were moving off to get food, find friends. . . Penny was seized by a strange kind of panic. Slowly she turned round, and found James standing almost directly behind her, regarding her with a roguish twinkle in his eyes. 'Ah, I was just debating whether the front of that dress was going to be more or less revealing than the back!'

She took another gulp of her drink. 'Disappointed?' she asked, tilting her chin to look him squarely in the eye.

He looked amused. 'Not at all—it's a wicked little dress. Very appropriate!'

Penny's colour rose. 'Appropriate for the brazen little hussy who's wearing it?'

'Ssh—there's no need to shout! How much of that stuff have you had to drink?' He peered into her half-empty glass.

'Not much—and it's none of your business, anyway.'

'What's got into you—oh, I forgot, you didn't want to come to the party if I was going to be here, did you? I suppose I've ruined your evening now.' His expression was serious, but there was still a gleam in his eye which Penny found irritating. 'I'll just go over here and we can pretend we haven't seen each other. . .'

The party was in full swing now. The french doors were flung wide open on to the garden, and several people had drifted outside to sit in the warm night air.

'Ladies and gentlemen. . .' Steven stood on a chair to gain everyone's attention, and the chatter gradually subsided.

'Thank you all for coming,' began Steven, looking a little embarrassed to have so many eyes upon him, 'especially, for many of you, at very short notice. I just want to wish my beautiful wife Jan a very happy birthday——' there was a pause while he planted a loving kiss on his wife's lips '—and to give her this, with all my love!'

He thrust a small gift-wrapped box into Jan's hand, and everyone craned their necks to watch as she unwrapped it and lifted the lid. She reached inside with a gasp, and held up a stunning, heavy gold bracelet. 'Oh, *Steven!*' she gasped, before flinging her arms around his neck. Everyone cheered, and Steven proposed a toast to his wife.

'To Jan!' echoed the guests. Penny lifted her glass and realised, to her surprise, that it was empty.

She felt suddenly and unaccountably depressed. All these happy couples, and she was alone. As usual. That was the only thing she missed about her relationship with Chris—the sense of belonging with someone. Except, of course, that he hadn't belonged with *her*.

She turned unsteadily and cannoned into James, who had been leaning against the open French door. He caught her by the elbows, holding her firmly until she had regained her balance.

'Goodness, how did I do that?' she muttered, looking up into his concerned face.

He was still holding her, but now he released her arms and caught hold of one hand, drawing her into the room where several couples were dancing to a slow, romantic record.

Everything was beginning to feel a little unreal. Dreamily, Penny allowed herself to settle into James's arms. She rested her head against his chest, and closed her eyes.

They moved together in time to the music. Penny was muzzily aware of James's hands caressing her waist, her hips, and then her eyes flew open as his fingers explored the naked skin of her back. Hot needles seemed to shoot from the nape of her neck down to her toes. She jerked her head up to meet his eyes—he looked back, half smiling.

'I thought that might wake you up!' he laughed. 'I must say, your skin feels absolutely delicious. . .' He was whispering into her ear now, and as he spoke his hands traced a path across her shoulder-blades and down her spine. Unable to bear this teasing, tempting intimacy a moment longer, she pulled away from his grasp.

'I—I think it's time I left,' she murmured. 'I'll go and find Jan—say goodbye——'

She finally discovered Jan and Steven cuddling together on a garden bench, looking relaxed and contented.

'You're not going already?' exclaimed Jan, as Penny thanked her for the evening.

'Yes, I think I should. I'm. . .a bit tired,' mumbled Penny, suddenly feeling overwhelmingly exhausted.

Steven looked concerned. 'You're not driving, are you?' he asked.

She forced a bright smile. 'Yes, of course. Why ever not?'

She turned to find her way barred by James. 'I'm taking you home,' he said quietly.

Trying to push him away, Penny glared at him. 'No, you are not—I've got my own car. . .'

James grabbed her by the wrist and kept her, wriggling, by his side. 'Penny, you're in no fit state to drive. You've had far too much to drink—you'll either kill yourself, or more likely someone else.' He kept his voice low, but every word went home. 'Just be sensible for once, and let me give you a lift to Fernhill. You can come back for your car tomorrow, when you're sober!'

'I am not *drunk*!' hissed Penny as he guided her out of the front door and into the passenger seat of his car. 'I've only had a couple of glasses of wine!'

'The quantity isn't important—you've had more than you can tolerate. Why were you drinking, anyway? It's not like you.'

Penny hung her head and pondered the question. 'I don't know—I think it had something to do with you. . .'

James pulled a face and glanced at her as he drove through the dark streets. 'Is that the effect I have on you—driving you to drink?'

'Something like that,' she muttered, closing her eyes and resting her head back against the seat. That made her feel sick, so she opened them again and sat forward, trying to see the road ahead. 'You've been following me around all evening like some sort of guardian angel— every time I turned around, there you were,' she complained. 'What was the big idea?'

James shrugged. 'If you're going to do stupid things

like getting drunk, then someone's got to be there to protect you from yourself.'

'I told you, I'm not drunk—just tired,' muttered Penny as they drew up outside Marsh Farm Cottage. 'Don't see me to the door—I can manage to walk up the path unaided!'

'OK—whatever you say!' James watched her, a spark of amusement in his eye, as she climbed unsteadily from the car. 'Goodnight, then—I hope your head isn't too painful in the morning!'

Penny was glad to find that her mother and grand-mother were both in bed. Thankfully, she stripped off her dress and fell into bed, wondering, before she sank into oblivion, why everything was spinning round. . .

CHAPTER TWELVE

'PENNY! Are you up yet?' Her mother's voice roused Penny from a fitful sleep. She lifted her head slightly and peered at the clock. Eleven-fifteen!

Groaning, she stumbled out of bed and opened her door. 'What's the matter?' she called feebly.

'There's a very nice young man down here who says he's brought you a hangover cure!'

Penny groaned again. 'Tell him to go away!' The noise of her own voice seemed to be splitting her head in two. Just what had she done to herself last night? She always prided herself on knowing her own limit with alcohol—what the hell had prompted her to overdo it?

A hot shower revived her a little, but not much. She pulled on her oldest and best-loved tracksuit and slowly made her way downstairs.

Her mother was sitting at the kitchen table with the Sunday papers and a cup of coffee. Penny fell into the chair opposite and looked longingly at Josephine's cup.

'If you want coffee, you'll have to get up and get it yourself. There's plenty in the pot.'

'You're a hard woman,' complained Penny, pouring out the strong black brew. 'Has James gone?'

'No—he's in the garden. You'd better take him another cup of coffee—he's been waiting a long time!'

Penny didn't feel up to objecting, and meekly filled another mug. 'What's all this about a hangover cure?' she asked, adding quickly, 'Not that I need one, of course?'

'You'll soon find out,' was all her mother would say,

smiling at her wan-faced daughter over the top of her spectacles.

It was another gorgeous day. The clear sky was a little hazy, promising a hot afternoon. The garden smelt of damp earth and newly cut grass, and Penny breathed deeply as she rounded the side of the house and stepped into the back garden.

James was stooping, hands clasped behind his back, to look at a spreading mat of geraniums in the herbaceous border. He wore faded jeans, trainers and a navy blue T-shirt, and his bare arms were already tanned.

'It's beautiful, isn't it?' Penny approached, holding out the coffee she had brought. 'Buxton's Blue—a stunning plant.'

'I didn't know you were a gardener.' James straightened up and looked down at her gravely.

'I'm not really, but I planted that one myself, last year. That's the only reason I remember its name.' She sat down on the grass and sipped her drink.

'You don't look capable of remembering your own name this morning! How are you feeling?'

Penny made a face at him. 'Fine, thank you. Would you mind just keeping your voice down a bit?'

He laughed, and shook his head at her. 'Oh, dear. If you will over-indulge, you must pay the price. Actually, I've got just the thing you need. It'll do you the world of good. Come and see. . .'

He held out his hand to help her up. The movement made her head thump, but she wasn't going to admit that to James Yorke. She scowled at him—he looked far too healthy for his own good, striding across the lawn towards the front of the cottage.

She followed a few yards behind, then stopped dead as she saw him standing beside two brightly coloured mountain bikes.

'What are those?' she demanded.

'I told you—your hangover cure!'

Penny came nearer, and shaded her eyes to look at the smaller of the two cycles, which was painted a vivid yellow and purple. 'OK, I feel better now. You can take it away——'

'Come on, try it out. The saddle might be too high. . .'

'Who does it belong to?' She wheeled it out into the lane and tried to get on, but she could barely reach the pedals.

James produced a spanner and set to work to adjust the height. 'It's Jan's—which accounts for the choice of colour! I borrowed it this morning. Here, try this.'

Penny felt too weak to argue. There seemed to be a huge weight pressing behind her eyes.

'Perhaps you could just explain to me what's going on—I seem to be a bit slow on the uptake this morning. . .'

James put his hands on her shoulders and looked into her face. 'We're going on a bike ride,' he said slowly and deliberately, his eyes twinkling. 'The fresh air will do you good. We can ride through the countryside, stop for a picnic, then cycle over to Ellminster to collect your car.'

'That'll be miles!' she protested.

'Not many. You'll manage.'

Penny looked doubtfully at the bicycle again, and sighed. 'I suppose I'd better go and change into something that doesn't clash with that awful machine—if that's possible!' Halfway back into the house she turned and looked at James. 'Why are you doing this?'

He shook his head. 'I'm beginning to wonder. . .'

Five minutes later she reappeared in navy bermuda shorts and a white cotton sleeveless blouse. From the appreciative look James gave her she guessed that her appearance was much improved.

They set off. The first few minutes were sheer hell for Penny. She seemed to feel every bump and stone in the road, and she was tempted to call to James to stop and let her go back. But he was quite a way ahead, and her pride wouldn't quite let her give up. She struggled on, and as they approached the next village, Oakley, she was beginning to enjoy the breeze in her face. She shook her head and was pleased to find that the dreadful pounding had ceased. James was waiting by the village green for her to catch up.

'How are you feeling now?' he asked.

'Great!' Penny smiled.

'Good, because we're going uphill from now on. Think you can manage a climb?'

'Of course. If you can do it, I'm sure I can.'

James laughed. 'We'll see who gets to the top first, then! Don't forget to use your gears.'

He led the way, off the village road and along a farm track. About a mile along, the track forked, and one branch led up a steep, steep hill. Penny gritted her teeth and followed James, but keeping up with him proved impossible. Despite the enormous number of gears, she couldn't manage to keep pedalling, and in the end she had to get off the bike and push it laboriously up the hillside.

At the top she found James, perched on an old log, his bicycle on the ground beside him. She pushed her bike over to him and dropped it down, panting loudly. James made room for her on the log. He was barely out of breath, she noticed with irritation.

'Just look at that view!' He was gazing into the distance. It was indeed a spectacular sight—miles of the Gloucestershire countryside spread out beneath them.

'Wow! Where's Fernhill?' Penny had lost her bearings, and James pointed her in the right direction.

'Look, there's Ellminster beyond, and that would be Gloucester in the distance, if you could see that far.'

She followed his pointing finger, her eyes narrowed against the sunlight. 'Thank you for bringing me up here, James. It's fantastic!'

'You're feeling better, then?'

'I feel wonderful!' Penny took a deep breath, filling her lungs with the sweet, grassy air. She breathed out slowly, closing her eyes and tipping her face up to the sun.

Watching her, unseen, James smiled slightly. 'I'm glad my cure worked so well,' he said at last.

She opened one eye and made a face at him. 'I don't know why you keep on about me being in such a bad way. I've never had a hangover in my life!'

James gave a deep chuckle. 'Really? When you staggered out into your garden this morning, I could have sworn——'

'OK, OK!' she interrupted, rolling her eyes. 'I confess I was feeling a bit delicate—but now. . .' She jumped up from the log and retrieved James's rucksack, which had been lying beside the bikes. 'Now I feel hungry!'

'Right, let's see what we have. . .' James fished about in the bag and produced bread rolls, cheese, fruit and two small bottles of mineral water.

Penny sat down on the grass to eat her lunch, marvelling at how such simple food could taste so special in the open air. 'That was excellent,' she said, finishing the last of the water, and lying down to enjoy the sun on her face.

For a few minutes there was silence, broken only by the cawing of the rooks in the trees behind them, and the faint hum of traffic from the road at the bottom of the hill.

'Where will you go when you leave the practice?'

James's unwelcome question intruded on Penny's carefree daydreaming, and she frowned. 'I don't know yet. Somewhere—anywhere!'

'Anywhere to get away from me?'

'I didn't say that.' It sounded ridiculous anyway, when they had just spent such an enjoyable couple of hours together. 'It's not just you, James——' She didn't know how to continue, and lapsed into silence. The pleasant atmosphere had evaporated.

'Penny——' James hesitated, looking down at his hands, spread out before him. 'I only want to know one thing. Were you—are you—in love with Kit?'

She stared at him, horrified. How could he ask such a question? 'You've got a damned nerve!' she snapped. 'How dare you pry into my feelings? You treat me like some cheap little tart, and then expect me to tell you whether or not I'm in love with your brother? It's got absolutely nothing to do with you!'

She leapt to her feet and hauled Jan's bike up from the ground.

'Penny, wait!' James was standing up too, but Penny was already pushing her bike across the grass, towards the track.

'Don't follow me!' she flung back over her shoulders. 'I don't want to see you!' Reaching the top of the lane, she hopped up on to the bike and began the downhill ride.

The wind whipped across her face as she sped down the steep track, but she welcomed it, glad of its cooling effect on her blazing cheeks. How could James have been so insensitive? Here she was, hopelessly in love with the man, and all he was interested in was her fateful relationship with Chris.

She pulled on the brakes, but she was still descending the hill at an alarming speed. Her stomach churned with excitement—it felt dangerous, exhilarating. It was exactly what she needed at this moment.

She had almost reached the fork in the lane before she realised she didn't know which way to turn for Ellminster. She intended to return Jan's bicycle and pick up her car, but for a moment her sense of direction deserted her, and so did her control of the bike. Instead of stopping at the foot of the track, she carried on, veering right out into the farm road. Desperately she tried to steer round to the left, but all that happened was that the wheels skidded and slipped from beneath her. The next thing she knew, she was sliding painfully across the gritty surface, leaving the bike on its side, several feet away, wheels spinning crazily.

She picked herself up slowly, wincing as she moved her badly grazed elbow and knee. Just as she got to her feet she heard the sound of an approaching vehicle. Forgetting the pain of her injuries, she hauled the bike upright and dragged it off the road just in time for the car to pass.

Shaken, she sat down on the grass verge to recover her nerves before setting off again for Ellminster. She drew her knees up to her chest and rested her head on her folded arms.

'Penny—thank God! Are you all right? Here, let me see. . .' James was on his knees beside her, gently taking her arm and investigating the damage to her elbow and knees. The skin had been torn off and her right knee was bleeding quite badly.

'How did you know——?'

'I watched you careering down the hill like a madwoman—and then I saw you skid out into the road, but I couldn't see any more—the trees were in the way. I followed as fast as I could, imagining the worst—oh, darling, thank goodness you're still in one piece!'

Penny was listening, bemused. For a moment she thought she was hearing things. James delved into his rucksack and produced the table napkin which had contained the bread. Deftly he ripped it up to form a makeshift bandage, which he wrapped around her knee.

'There, that should stop the bleeding until I can get it cleaned up properly.'

'Thank you, Doctor! I suppose it's my own fault, running away like that.' Penny sighed miserably.

James shook his head. 'I don't blame you—I drove you away with my stupid, clumsy questions.' He sat down beside her on the grass, his arms folded on his knees. 'That's what jealousy does for you—turns you into the kind of person you never wanted to be.'

'You mean—you were jealous? Of whom?'

'Of my own brother, I'm ashamed to say. I fell in love with you, Penny, the day we met—the day you threw me out of your grandmother's house without letting me see her! But you seemed so frightened of making any kind of commitment, so I waited patiently. Then along came Kit. . .'

'And you discovered my secret. After that, you couldn't stand the sight of me. . .'

James closed his eyes, flung back his head, and gave a hollow laugh. 'I don't know where you got that idea from—but it did rather turn everything upside down. It's hard to discover that your own brother is a rival.'

'So that's why you wanted to know how I felt about him?' Penny was frowning, trying to keep a grip on reality, while her heart pounded wildly.

'Yes. You're about to disappear from my life, Penny—

run off to goodness knows where. In my blundering fashion I'm trying to find out whether there's still a chance for us.'

Penny sat in silence for a minute or two, struggling to make sense of everything. James had loved her—and perhaps still did? It seemed too much to hope for. . .

'I'm not in love with your brother,' she said carefully. 'I thought I was, at first—before I knew he was married—but now I realise that I didn't really love him at all.'

'What makes you say that?'

She took a deep breath. 'Because when I met you, I discovered the real thing. It's painful, it's miserable, and it won't go away!'

'Yup, that's love all right!' said James, grinning broadly. 'There's a very good treatment for the side effects. . .'

Tenderly he cupped her face in his hands and gently kissed her forehead, her eyelids, her nose, her cheeks. At last he claimed her lips with a sweet, slow kiss which seemed to spread a healing warmth through Penny's whole body.

'Better?' he asked at last.

She nodded, smiling shyly. 'Much.'

'Penny, tell me why you thought I wanted you out of the way once I knew about Kit?'

She frowned, puzzled. 'It was obvious. You hated the woman who'd broken up your brother's marriage. You threw me out of your house that night. . .'

James winced at the memory. 'I was shocked, yes, but I didn't hate you, Penny. How could I—I was desperately in love with you! It was Kit I was furious with, and I don't mind admitting I put him through hell that weekend. By the time we'd finished, I had a very clear picture of what had gone on in London. I tried to talk to you at the surgery, to apologise for sending you away, but you seemed so determined to believe that I despised you. I suspected it was because you still cared for Kit.'

'Oh, no!' Penny shook her head. 'You mean—you didn't blame me?'

'Of course not. I know I'm over-protective about Kit, but I'm not completely stupid. Well, perhaps I am. I certainly made myself thoroughly miserable, thinking the worst. Especially when I saw you together at the station. . .'

Penny laughed, remembering her final conversation with Chris. 'What a pity you weren't standing within earshot—you would have heard your brother discovering that I was in love with you!'

'Am I the last to know?' teased James.

She pretended to consider, counting on her fingers. 'Probably—let's see now, there's my grandmother, my mother, Chris, Jan. . .'

'Have you been talking to Jan?' chuckled James. 'Poor girl—between the two of us, she must be bored to tears with our problems!'

'Don't tell me you've been crying on her shoulder as well?'

He aimed a playful cuff at her ear. 'Something like that. Which reminds me—hadn't we better try and get you reunited with your car?'

Painfully Penny stood up. Her damaged knees ached, and her elbow felt stiff.

'How far is it to Ellminster?' she asked.

'A couple of miles. Will you be able to ride?'

'I think so, if we take it slowly.'

They set off, cycling side by side along the farm lane towards the main road. 'I hope you're not still thinking of leaving,' said James.

'Maybe—maybe not,' teased Penny. 'What would you like me to do?'

'I was rather hoping you'd stay here and marry me, darling.'

She wobbled to a halt, and James stopped a few feet ahead, turning to frown with concern. 'What's wrong?' he demanded.

Penny smiled, her hazel eyes glinting with mischief. 'I suddenly feel rather weak—I think I need another dose of your special treatment!'

— MEDICAL ROMANCE —

The books for enjoyment this month are:

RAW DEAL Caroline Anderson
A PRIVATE ARRANGEMENT Lilian Darcy
SISTER PENNY'S SECRET Clare Mackay
SURGEON FROM FRANCE Elizabeth Petty

♥　♥　♥　♥　♥

Treats in store!

Watch next month for the following absorbing stories:

KNAVE OF HEARTS Caroline Anderson
OUT OF PRACTICE Lynne Collins
MONSOONS APART Sheila Danton
SEEDS OF LOVE Margaret O'Neill

Available from Boots, Martins, John Menzies, W.H. Smith, most supermarkets and other paperback stockists.

Also available from Mills & Boon Reader Service, P.O. Box 236, Thornton Road, Croydon, Surrey CR9 3RU.

Readers in South Africa - write to:
Book Services International Ltd, P.O. Box 41654, Craighall, Transvaal 2024.

Love is in the Air...

Mills & Boon have commissioned four of your favourite authors to write four tender romances.

uaranteed love and excitement for St. Valentine's Day

A BRILLIANT DISGUISE	-	Rosalie Ash
FLOATING ON AIR	-	Angela Devine
THE PROPOSAL	-	Betty Neels
VIOLETS ARE BLUE	-	Jennifer Taylor

vailable from January 1993   PRICE £3.99

 Mills & Boon

*Available from Boots, Martins, John Menzies, W.H. Smith,
most supermarkets and other paperback stockists.
Also available from Mills & Boon Reader Service, PO Box 236,
Thornton Road, Croydon, Surrey CR9 3RU.*

THE PERFECT GIFT FOR MOTHER'S DAY

Specially selected for you -
four tender and heartwarming
Romances written by popular
authors.

LEGEND OF LOVE -
Melinda Cross

AN IMPERFECT AFFAIR -
Natalie Fox

LOVE IS THE KEY -
Mary Lyons

LOVE LIKE GOLD -
Valerie Parv

Available from February 1993   Price: £6.80

*Available from Boots, Martins, John Menzies, W.H. Smith,
most supermarkets and other paperback stockists.
Also available from Mills & Boon Reader Service, PO Box 236,
Thornton Road, Croydon, Surrey CR9 3RU.
(UK Postage & Packing free)*

Mills & Boon

Discover the thrill of 4 Exciting
Medical Romances – FREE

FREE
BOOKS FOR YOU

In the exciting world of modern
medicine, the emotions of true love
have an added drama. Now you can
experience four of these
unforgettable romantic tales of passion
and heartbreak FREE – and look forward to
a regular supply of Mills & Boon
Medical Romances delivered direct to your door!

❧ ❧ ❧

Turn the page for details of 2 extra
free gifts, and how to apply.

An Irresistible Offer from Mills & Boon

Here's an offer from Mills & Boon to become a regular reader of Medical Romances. To welcome you, we'd like you to have four books, a cuddly teddy and a special MYSTERY GIFT, all absolutely free and without obligation.

Then, every month you could look forward to receiving 4 more **brand new** Medical Romances for £1.70 each, delivered direct to your door, post and packing free. Plus our newsletter featuring author news, competitions, special offers, and lots more.

This invitation comes with no strings attached. You can cancel or suspend your subscription at any time, and still keep your free books and gifts.

Its so easy. Send no money now. Simply fill in the coupon below and post it at once to -

Mills & Boon Reader Service, FREEPOST, PO Box 236, Croydon, Surrey CR9 9EL

NO STAMP REQUIRED

✂ -

YES! Please rush me my 4 Free Medical Romances and 2 Free Gifts! Please also reserve me a Reader Service Subscription. If I decide to subscribe, I can look forward to receiving 4 brand new Medical Romances every month for just £6.80, delivered direct to my door. Post and packing is free, and there's a free Mills & Boon Newsletter. If I choose not to subscribe I shall write to you within 10 days - I can keep the books and gifts whatever I decide. I can cancel or suspend my subscription at any time. I am over 18.

EP20D

Name (Mr/Mrs/Ms) _____

Address _____

_____

_____ Postcode _____

Signature _____

The right is reserved to refuse an application and change the terms of this offer. Offer expires 28th February 1993. Readers in Southern Africa write to Book Services International Ltd, P.O. Box 41654, Craighall, Transvaal 2024. Other Overseas and Eire, send for details. You may be mailed with other offers from Mills & Boon and other reputable companies as a result of this application. If you would prefer not to share in this opportunity, please tick box. ☐